Holy Murder

Rodney Hobson

First published 2014 by Endeavour Press Ltd.

This edition published 2018 by Sharpe Books.

Table of Contents

Chapter 1 9

Chapter 2 12

Chapter 3 15

Chapter 4 18

Chapter 5 23

Chapter 6 29

Chapter 7 35

Chapter 8 38

Chapter 9 43

Chapter 10 48

Chapter 11 52

Chapter 12 56

Chapter 13 60

Chapter 14 63

Chapter 15 69

Chapter 16 76

Chapter 17 79

Chapter 18...83

Chapter 19...86

Chapter 20...90

Chapter 21...93

Chapter 22...97

Chapter 23...105

Chapter 24...111

Chapter 25...114

Chapter 26...119

Chapter 27...123

Chapter 28...128

Chapter 29...132

Chapter 30...138

Chapter 31...142

Chapter 32...145

Chapter 33...148

Chapter 34...151

Chapter 35...155

Chapter 36...158

Chapter 37...162

Chapter 38 167

Chapter 39 170

Chapter 40 173

Chapter 41 176

Chapter 42 178

Chapter 43 184

Chapter 1

The bells in the Stump began to ring as Simeon Knowles and Dr Lesley Austin made their way up the 209 steps to the walkway high on the famous tower of Boston's parish church.

Across miles of flat land and out across the Wash, the bells were intended to be clearly audible to guide ships to the Haven or warn peasants of floods or pirates; inside the tower they were a deafening racket unbearable to the human ear.

Even Knowles, hard of hearing as he was, could not cope with the assault on his auditory senses; two officials already higher up, much less so. They all came scurrying down, hands over ears, Dr Austin actually colliding with Knowles and sending him sprawling.

As they reached the comparative calm of the nave, a churchwarden hurried up to them, full of apologies that they could hardly hear as the incessant ringing continued in their heads. Spectators, organisers and church officials milled round, their anxious voices a whirl of noise.

Knowles, Dr Austin and the two leaders of the Fens Abseiling Club who had been stationed on the walkway two thirds of the way up the Stump slowly recovered their breath and their hearing. Being by far the eldest at 75, Knowles took longer to return to equilibrium.

It was Gail Westerham, chairman and leading light of the abseiling society, who let forth an ungodly expression that rang up to what was once the highest roof of any building in the world. The churchwarden and a group of American tourists stepped back, shocked. Other

9

visitors and members of the public supporting the *Stump Up* charity event that had brought abseilers to the church milled round.

Eventually the bell ringing stopped. A few moments later, a small, muscular man panting a little from exertion, bustled through from the tower wringing his hands.

"Terribly sorry. Didn't realise we'd cause such a fuss. Never anybody up the tower usually when we ring the bells. Didn't know it would be so deafening."

"For goodness sake, man," Westerham exploded, while keeping control of her language, "how did you think it would sound? What the hell were you playing at anyway?"

"The Brides of Mavis Enderby," the bell ringer replied, deadpan.

"It's a peal of bells," the churchwarden explained briefly.

This ludicrous exchange diffused the situation sufficiently for Westerham to turn her back on church officials and regroup her battered troops.

"Are we all ready to go up again?" she asked, adding pointedly: "I'm sure there will be no more interruptions. We have lost enough time already."

Knowles was already on his feet, talking to well-wishers and showing off the harness that he had already donned for his descent of the outside of the tower before being so rudely interrupted.

Dr Austin took him by the arm and steered him back to the steps, which were now ringing only with the footsteps of Westerham and her abseiling club colleague leading the way. It had been fully a quarter of an hour between the last descent of the tower and the emergence of Simeon Knowles to make the next one.

Knowles looked down from the walkway and was gratified to see a large throng on the opposite bank of the river, which was little more than a trickle. Spectators had apparently not dispersed during the unscheduled delay. Directly below, two members of the abseiling club waited to receive him.

He stretched out his arms and stood framed against the lantern tower that formed the uppermost part of the Stump. Then he turned majestically, sat on the edge of the low wall round the walkway and eased back.

Soon he was fully outside the tower, leaning back and letting his feet take the weight of his short, stocky body on the wall.

Suddenly, and without warning, the harness gave way.

Knowles plunged, his body flat out as it had been in his last moments attached to the rope that had secured him to the tower. The two abseiling club members doing duty at the base of the tower, whose role was to remove the harness at the end of each descent, leapt aside, one throwing himself over the wall into the mud at the edge of the river.

Knowles hit the ground like a sack of potatoes with a sickening thud. Then there came the squelching of mud as the club member pulled himself up onto the river bank wall and stared, frozen with horror, at his fellow abseiler.

The two of them slowly turned their eyes and gazed at the motionless body lying flat between them.

The quiet was broken by a shrill cry from the riverbank.

"Oh no! Not Simeon. Not Simeon. The man's a saint!"

Chapter 2

Detective Inspector Paul Amos was just about to leave home to go shopping in Lincoln with his wife to find summer clothes for their 1993 annual holiday when the phone rang. He and Mrs Amos both raised their eyes to the ceiling at the intrusion. It was Mrs Amos who spoke.

"Go on, you'd better answer it. It could be important."

Given the marital consent despite this being his day off duty, Amos picked up the phone after a moment's hesitation.

"We could have left the house already," he suggested as he reached across for the receiver. The couple were in the hall, debating whether they needed to take macs. His wife shook her head. He lifted the receiver.

"Amos here."

"Fletcher here," barked out the voice at the other end.

Amos nearly dropped the phone. His wife raised her eyebrows. She could hear the voice of the Chief Constable of Lincolnshire clearly enough from three feet away.

"Sir," Amos said simply.

"Amos, this is serious. I need a top man on this, someone I can trust."

Amos and his wife, who could hear clearly, looked at each other in surprise.

"Unfortunately," Sir Robert Fletcher went on, "Johnson is away on holiday so it will have to be you. So just listen. This has to be handled carefully. Simeon Knowles has been killed in an accident at St Botolph's Church in Boston. It has to be an accident but I want whoever was responsible to be held to account. I need you down there pronto to sort things out.

"The Boston squad are keeping everybody involved together until you can get there but I can't trust them to handle something like this. It's only their Saturday team anyway and they'll never cope. Get a squad car and move as fast as you can."

"Forgive me, sir, but I take it this Simeon chap is known to you. Who is he?"

"Amos, you're wasting valuable time. He's big in the county, big in charity work, big in local society, big in golfing circles. Need I say more?"

And big in the Freemasons, too, Amos thought.

"I'm on my way, sir."

Amos put the phone down before Fletcher could berate his tardiness further. He looked anxiously at his wife but she was taking it all rather calmly.

"Don't worry," she said, "I'll get on better on my own. I won't feel you are hanging round bored while I buy clothes. Will you have time to drop me in the centre or is it really urgent?"

"Just give me a moment and I'll drop you near the Castle if you don't mind walking down the hill. The late and apparently lamented Simeon, or whatever he was called, can hang on. The Boston station guys are fine."

His wife nodded her assent.

"Juliet's on duty today. I'll get her in a squad car waiting for me."

13

Amos rang headquarters at Nettleham on the east side of Lincoln and made arrangements with Detective Sergeant Juliet Swift. She was in the car park waiting, engine running, when Amos arrived after a short detour that would have given the Chief Constable apoplexy had he known.

Swift knew she would be driving. She could handle speed better than Amos. Within half an hour, blue lights flashing and siren blaring, they were in Boston market place, parking on double yellow lines.

Chapter 3

Detective Sergeant Gerry Burnside of Boston CID was in charge, as Amos and Swift soon discovered after they forced their way through a crowd of people and strode under the statue of the town's patron saint atop the south door and into the parish church of St Botolph's.

Amos was not sorry to see Burnside. Although he was a bit of a plodder, rarely given to bouts of inspiration let alone genius, he was extremely efficient and well organised, never one to panic under pressure.

Burnside greeted Amos cheerfully.

"I got here within five minutes of the incident, Sir," he told Amos. "Someone from the church had the presence of mind to phone immediately after it happened and the police station is only just across the river. I nipped over the footbridge. I've managed to corral just about everyone directly involved and a few more besides. Better to err on the side of caution, that's my motto."

"Quite right, sergeant," Amos responded smoothly. "Can you give us a quick run through in private first."

"Absolutely," Burnside enthused. "I've managed to commandeer the vestry as a temporary incident room. Let's go in there."

Amos concurred. He looked round. A couple of dozen people had settled with varying degrees of impatience and annoyance in the pews. An air of shock, as much as the efficiency of the Boston constabulary, had kept them in check.

Once in the privacy of the vestry, Burnside started to sketch in such details as he had already ascertained.

"I've concentrated on the people who were actually in the church," he explained. "There were quite a number on the road across the river but they were soon joined by dozens of gawking ghouls so it was impossible to judge who was there at the time, who had left and who had joined the throng since.

"In any case, they were well away from the action so there didn't seem much point, although I reckon someone could just about have been in the church when the victim started his ascent, nipped down to the edge of the Market Place, crossed the bridge and trotted up the other side of the Witham by the time the victim reached the top."

"You did absolutely right, Gerry," Amos assured him smoothly. "What do you gather happened, here in the church?"

"I'm told it was an event organised by the Fens Abseiling Club. It was some sort of charity event. As you can imagine, the Stump has iconic status in these parts so it was a bit of a coup for the club to get permission to scale down it."

"Was it just club members doing the descent?"

"As far as I can gather it was a mixture of club members and public show-offs. Some people, including the chair and vice-chair of the club, had already made the descent, attracting a decent sized crowd on the far river bank because they were so visible.

"The dead man is Simeon Knowles," Burnside continued, after a glance at his notebook. Apparently the significance of the name as a personal friend of the Chief Constable and as a general do-gooder had not registered with the detective sergeant, any more than it had with Amos.

"He fell from the top. It was definitely not an accident. According to at least three members of the abseiling club who have seen the harness since, it had been tampered with, presumably within the church."

"That should narrow it down a bit," Amos commented. "Surely very few people would have had the opportunity. I take it there is no doubt that it was deliberate sabotage?"

"I'm assured that this was definitely sabotage. Unfortunately the list of possible perpetrators is wider than you might think. At some point just before Knowles went up to his doom, the bell ringers started a peal of bells. Club members up the Stump were forced to abandon their posts or face permanent deafness.

"There was a lot of chaos and milling about while the matter was resolved. Quite a number of people had the opportunity to intervene. No-one would have particularly noticed if a complete stranger had wandered up in the middle of the melee.

"However, there are certain people who stand out more than most. Three club members" – again Burnside consulted his notes for the names – "Gail Westerham, Mike Tate and Lesley Austin, plus the church warden and the chief bell-ringer are the main suspects. But other members of the abseiling club would have gone unnoticed and would have had knowledge of how the harness worked."

"OK," Amos decided. "We'll take the two head honchos from the abseiling club first, then Austin. After that we'll go for the church warden and the chief bell-ringer. Do you think you and your team could get statements from the others who were on the scene and let them go, Gerry? Hang on to any who look more interesting or whose address you can't verify."

17

Chapter 4

Detective Inspector Paul Amos and Detective Sergeant Juliet Swift decided to split the two leaders of the Fens Abseiling Club between them, partly to save time and partly so that their respective stories could be gathered with the least danger that they might collude.

Swift was allocated the vestry, which had been vacated to make a temporary incident and interview room, and Mike Tate, who was the Fens Abseiling Club's second in command. Amos settled for a pew in a quiet corner of the church but kept the club leader, Gail Westerham, for himself.

"Tell me about the club," Amos asked her. "It seems to me rather odd that a club whose purpose is to scale down vertical drops should be based in the flattest part of the county."

Westerham gave a short, nervous laugh.

"I suppose it is," she admitted. "Well, yes, that was the point in a way. We all wanted a bit of excitement and scaling buildings and cliffs gave us days out. We've done one or two weekends away as well."

"And church towers?"

"Occasionally. We make a donation and it attracts people to the church so vicars are often quite relaxed about it."

"And Boston Stump?"

"We were really excited when we got permission to do it. You know this is the second largest parish church in the country? And, of course, the Stump is famous. You can see it for miles around. It's easily the biggest challenge we have had, no wonder everyone was so excited. We were sure of a big crowd and piles of publicity."

Exciting? Amos thought to himself. *Exciting? Watching abseiling makes snooker look exciting.* He decided not to voice his thoughts.

Instead he prompted: "Who's idea was it?"

Westerham thought for a moment.

"Well, actually, I think it was Simeon who first mentioned the idea. Mike – Mike Tate – brought it up at a meeting but I'm pretty sure he said that Simeon had put the idea to him. The church council were a bit reluctant at first but when we offered to raise money through sponsorship and running a collection among spectators on the day, they came round, some with more enthusiasm than others.

"We agreed that the proceeds would be divided equally between the Stump restoration fund and distressed farmers within the parish and neighbouring parishes. That persuaded the reluctant ones to see reason."

"I take it that Simeon Knowles is – was – a member of your club," Amos interjected. "Is there an age limit?"

"No and no," Westerham replied. "Simeon was not a member, although he had done one church tower with us in the past, the one at West Keal on the edge of the ridge. Funnily enough, the tower top is the same height above sea level as the Stump, although the drop is nothing like as far because it's on the ridge.

"And no, there is no age limit. It is all about fitness, physical and mental. Simeon passes with flying colours on both counts. On the rare occasions we allow members of the public to take part we always have a doctor on hand to check them over.

"Dr Austin does the honours. She was here today doing her stuff. She checked that Simeon was OK, although it was pretty much a formality."

"OK, she checked him from a health point of view," Amos accepted. "What about his harness? Who, if anyone, checked that? And by the way," he interjected as Gail Westerham opened her mouth to reply, "if in fact no-one checked it, it's better to say so now because we will find out."

"Dr Austin said she'd checked it at the bottom of the steps," Westerham replied, a little testily. "She helped him put it on. We always make safety a top priority, and, if you'll pardon my saying so, I resent the suggestion that we fell down in our duty to a member of the public on this occasion."

Amos ignored Westerham's pique and pressed on: "Where were you when everything happened?"

Westerham sniffed but replied: "Mike and I were at the top of the Stump, on the walkway. We were lowering down a club member and looking out for the next abseiler to come up the steps. Then the bells started ringing out right next to us. Luckily the person we were lowering – I think it was Jill Saunders – was just about at the bottom.

"We abandoned our post as soon as we were sure she was safe, which was only a matter of seconds, but enough to nearly deafen us for life. Then we scrambled down the steps. Near the bottom we collided with Dr Austin and Simeon Knowles, who had started to make the ascent but turned back when the bells started ringing. Knowles was the next one due to make the drop."

"How long were you down in the church before you went back up again?"

Gail Westerham thought for a long time.

"Do you know," she finally replied, "I'm really not sure. I didn't look at my watch before we were disturbed because you have to concentrate on what you are doing – and you get a bit carried away with the excitement, even after all the years I have been doing it. Boston Stump was our crowning moment.

"There was all the palaver about getting the bell ringing stopped. I don't really know how long it all took. Probably about a quarter of an hour, maybe a bit less. I did look at my watch when we got back to the top and reckoned we were running a good 20 to 25 minutes behind schedule at that point. But of course we also lost time on the stairs."

"Did you and the others stay in a group with Simeon Knowles?"

"Yes … no … well, sort of," came the uncertain reply from Westerham. "We did and we didn't, if you see what I mean."

Amos's faced indicated that he didn't see what she meant and the club leader attempted to explain: "We were sort of in a group but we didn't stick together all the time. We were talking to the church warden to find out what was going on and then one of the bell ringers came in so we weren't all together in a huddle all the time.

"Also we had to move at one point because we were blocking the entrance and exit to the church and there were visitors coming and going. Some of our equipment was in the way so we had to shift to one side to let people through.

"And a few tourists came up to ask us what was happening and whether we'd finished the abseiling. There was an American family who were very interested, heaven knows why.

"God, what a mess," she said suddenly and vehemently. "Simeon was such a good man. He'd help anyone in need and always stepped forward if you needed a volunteer."

"Presumably at some point the bells stopped ringing," Amos interposed swiftly, not wishing to allow Gail Westerham to lose her focus on the events leading up to the misadventure.

"Yes, the churchwarden scurried off to deal with it and then he and one of the bell-ringers came through and apologised. That's when we went back up the Stump."

"Who went back up?"

"Me, Mike Tate, Dr Austin and Simeon."

"Did you all go up together?" Amos asked.

"Yes, pretty much. We had to go in single file. I went first and the others followed. I can't say we all stuck together all the way up but we didn't rush and there wasn't much between us at the top. Lesley – that's Dr Austin – gave Simeon a quick check over, then he got onto the parapet round the walkway and leaned backwards. That's when it happened."

Gail Westerham, who had been quite calm and composed up to this point, suddenly broke down and buried her face in her hands.

Amos spoke to her gently: "Please take your time to recover. I shan't need to talk to you again today. I believe that the Boston police noted your address."

Westerham nodded passively and Amos stepped back to see how Swift had fared.

Chapter 5

Detective Sergeant Juliet Swift had not emerged from the vestry by the time that Paul Amos had completed his interview with Gail Westerham, nor was there any sign of Mike Tate, Westerham's number two. Perhaps Swift was making progress.

Best not to interrupt them, Amos thought. Instead he found Dr Lesley Austin, the doctor who had been with Simeon Knowles in the minutes leading up to his demise.

Dr Austin was in her forties, short haired and bespectacled, about 5 feet 8 inches tall and slightly built. Her medicine bag was at her feet in the front pew. She, more than Gail Westerham, seemed to have recovered her composure quite quickly.

"I've seen death before," she explained to Amos. "Trust me, I'm a doctor."

"Why were you here?" Amos asked. "Was it just to take part or were you in the church on duty as a doctor?"

"Both, inspector," Austin replied smoothly. "I am a keen abseiler myself, medical commitments permitting, and since we usually turn out at weekends when the surgery is closed, that means pretty much whenever I feel like it, which is quite often."

"Did you abseil down the Stump?"

"Yes, I went first. I always do whenever we allow members of the public to take part in a charity event like this one. I check all the participants before they make their ascent for blood pressure and to see if they are generally in good shape. We don't want anyone having a heart attack half way up or down."

Amos eyed her to see if this was an attempt at black humour. Dr Austin stared back coldly.

"And what shape was Simeon Knowles in?"

"Pretty good for his age, actually," Dr Austin pronounced. "Blood pressure just a little high before we went up the second time, hardly surprising given that we were half way up the Stump when those lunatics started ringing those bloody bells and we had to come back down and start up all over again when someone had shut them up.

"He was fine when I checked him before we set off the first time. Perfectly normal. He was obviously pretty fit. Breathing absolutely normal. Second time his blood pressure was up a little and his breathing was slightly faster but nothing out of the ordinary. Ditto at the top, but again well within the bounds of tolerance. He would have had no difficulty coming down."

"So you were with him at the bottom and then you walked up to the top with him?" Amos asked.

"That's right."

"You must be pretty fit yourself. Surely you didn't walk up and down with every person taking part. How many people were there scheduled to make the descent?"

"About 20," Dr Austin said, after a moment's mental reckoning. "We usually allow more if it's an ordinary church tower – in fact as many as want the thrill of risking their necks. But with this being such a steep climb up and a long drop we restricted the numbers and vetted the applicants. I can't be sure how many were going to do it because there's always one or two who chicken out, especially from such a height."

"Did anyone chicken out?" Amos asked.

"We'll never know," Austin replied. "It was too early in the day. I'd done the descent and so had Gail and a couple of our own members. Simeon Knowles was fifth in line and the first non-member to make the descent."

"Was that deliberate? Had he asked to go sooner rather than later? How was the running order selected?"

"He'd put his name down first when we opened up the list. It was typical of him to lead the way. He was very keen to show he wasn't an old fogey. He's well known in the fens for his voluntary work and raising money for good causes. A great many people have reason to be grateful to him, here and abroad."

"In what way?" Amos asked, his curiosity aroused.

"They say charity begins at home," Austin replied. "Simeon Knowles believed it began – and continued and never ended – at home and abroad. He's given financial support to a lot of struggling farmers in this area, and I mean really struggling. And he's also supported collections for orphanages in Eastern Europe where kids have been abandoned after the collapse of the Soviet Empire. So it was typical of him to be first to step forward when we decided to abseil down the Stump to raise funds for its restoration."

"Who approached him to take part? Or did he come to the club? Did he say how he had heard about it?"

"I approached him," Austin said in a matter of fact tone. "I knew he'd be keen and it got the list started. He knows people in the local press so he got us good publicity in the Boston edition of the *Standard*. Hence the big turnout of spectators. All down to him."

"Who, if anyone, checked his safety harness? I assume it was checked?"

Austin bridled a little at the implication that the abseiling club's negligence could have led to Knowles's demise.

"Of course it was checked," she countered sharply. "I was responsible for seeing that everything was in order – and it was. As a matter of fact," she went on, "it was the same harness that I had used, so I knew it was OK."

"Perhaps, then, you didn't check it as rigorously as you might have done," Amos persisted. "Perhaps you assumed it was all right because you yourself had used it without incident already."

Austin was now getting really hot under the collar at the clear pointing of the finger of guilt.

"How dare you," she responded angrily, rising to her feet. "I checked the harness properly and carefully. It was in perfect order."

The words came out slowly, deliberately, forcefully.

Amos backed down in the face of the vocal gale.

"Please understand, Dr Austin," he said quietly, "I must explore all avenues and grasp precisely what happened. I have to ascertain whether this was an unfortunate mishap caused by faulty equipment or human error, or if something deliberate happened here today. If it was human error it is better to establish that now rather than later."

Austin stood for a few moments before deciding that she had made her point. She subsided back into the pew.

"At what point did you check the harness? Was it before the first ascent, before the second, or at the top?"

26

"Simeon put the harness on at the bottom. It was something he wanted to do so that everyone could see the event was taking place. I checked the equipment at that point and it was fine. I didn't check it again as it didn't occur to me that there was any need to do so."

"I gather a lot of people were milling about after you were forced out of the tower by the bell ringing. Who could have got at the harness in the meantime before you went back up?"

"Well I was there, obviously," Austin said thoughtfully. "Gail Westerham and Mike Tate from the club – they were the ones on duty at the top. They came down when that racket began, but I don't think they knew Simeon particularly. I can't see why they would want to harm him.

"There was someone from the church fussing round but he went off to find the bell-ringers. Then one of the ringers came out. But there were loads of other people. Two or three other church officials, I think, spectators and tourists. The place was quite crowded. Oh, and there was a family of American tourists.

"When we went up the second time there were a few waifs and strays on the stairs who shouldn't have been there but they got through in the confusion. We had to push past them pretty closely and send them back down.

"Quite frankly, a lot of people had the opportunity to tamper with the harness, though whoever it was needed to know what they were doing. It had to be effective but not readily obvious otherwise we would have spotted it at the top of the Stump when the line was attached."

"Who was at the top? And would they have rechecked the harness?"

"Gail and Mike. No, their role was to make sure the rope was properly attached to the harness. In any case, I went up with Simeon as an extra precaution because of his age so if anyone had rechecked the harness it would have been me."

"But you didn't. Recheck it, that is?"

"There was no reason to. I didn't know someone had tampered with it in all the confusion."

Amos thought for a few moments. Then he asked suddenly: "You wore the same harness? Is there any possibility that it was tampered with before *you* wore it? Could someone have attempted to kill you, not Simeon Knowles? You don't weigh as much as he did so it might have just held."

Austin laughed. "Not a chance. Gail and Mike both checked it after I put it on. We were up on the walkway at the time so no-one had a chance to tamper with it after that."

"But Gail and Mike both had the opportunity?"

"Take my word for it, they couldn't have touched it without the other seeing. "

"It seems to me," Amos said warily, expecting an explosion, "that you were the one person with the best opportunity of deliberately killing Simeon Knowles."

"I'm sure that's right," Austin replied calmly. "If I were in your shoes I'd put me at the top of the suspect list. Well, you know where to find me," she added, "at least on weekdays. I'll be at my surgery."

Chapter 6

Amos was more than half way through his interview with Dr Austin by the time his detective sergeant Juliet Swift emerged from the vestry with a clearly distressed Mike Tate.

Swift hesitated for a few moments after passing Tate into the comforting arms of a woman and teenage girl, before taking a church official through to the vestry. She glanced towards Amos but, seeing him still engrossed with the doctor, decided to plough on with the next interview.

It was now Amos's turn to come clear and he looked round. The church was beginning to thin out as the Boston team worked their way efficiently through the crowd and ushered out the least likely prospects. Some visitors, relishing their moment at the heart of the action, were departing reluctantly.

Amos wandered up to Detective Sergeant Gerry Burnside.

"We're getting through pretty well," Burnside said. "It's much the same story as far as I can gather. Some people were here for the abseiling, but mostly it was tourists. Those who wanted to see the descent would be outside across the river. Either way, they all say there was a commotion soon after the bells started pealing, a lot of shouting and arguing.

"Then the bells stopped and a man came through fussing and all apologetic – he's the chief bell-ringer, although most people didn't know that, not being parishioners here. He came over to the group near the entrance to the Stump and there was a lot of fussing about, arguing and apologising loudly.

"Not everybody's story is identical because people were in different parts of the church and didn't see it all, but it all gels."

"Thanks, Gerry," Amos said. "Good result for Boston United yesterday, by the way. I'll take the chief bell-ringer if you and your team could take the other campanologists."

"Fine. Yes, they struggle a bit away from home. Haven't managed to come from behind to win all season. We've actually started on a couple of bell-ringers but we thought you'd want the guy in charge as he was the only one of them who came down into the church as far as we can see."

The chief bell-ringer gave his name as Herbert Townsend – Townsend without an H, he stressed. Townsend was a fussy little man, short and stout with muscular arms, which Amos could see protruding from a short sleeved shirt.

"I can't believe this has happened in a place of God," he blurted out, wringing his hands. "This, a place of sanctuary. How could God allow such a terrible accident to happen, here of all places?"

"How indeed," Amos observed dryly, hoping to stem the pointless lamentations.

Townsend, however, pressed on undeterred.

"Boston Stump has stood through the ages as a beacon to sailors, a refuge from pirates, a gathering place for those fleeing from persecution to seek a new life in America ..."

This rewriting of history was more than Amos could stomach.

"I think you'll find it was establishments like this that were doing the persecuting," he said curtly. "However, shall we get back to the matter in hand?"

The rebuke stunned Townsend, who sat sulkily.

"Did you arrive at the church before or after the abseiling started?"

"Before."

"Did you speak to anyone?"

"Yes."

Amos rolled his eyes up to the ceiling, seeking patience rather than God.

"Shall we try to be cooperative and get this over with, Mr Townsend?" he asked sharply. "When did you arrive and what happened. In your own words."

"I got here about quarter to 10," Townsend replied, with the bad grace of a schoolboy who has been chastised in front of the class. "I spoke to Dr Austin and watched the abseilers sorting their stuff out. When the first group set off up the tower I wandered through to the belfry to wait for the other bell-ringers."

"Did you notice anybody acting suspiciously?"

"Not really. Mind you, there was hardly anyone around at that time. In fact, I was rather surprised when I came out later – when there was all the commotion about the bell ringing – to see so many people milling about. There were a lot more people than usual for a Saturday morning."

"Was it normal to ring the bells on a Saturday morning? Was this bell practice?" Amos asked.

"Good Lord, no," Townsend replied, in a tone that suggested everyone should know when and where church bells were rung. "Not

31

unless there was a wedding and they were willing to pay for us. We have our own lives to lead, you know."

"Then why were you there?"

"Dr Austin asked us to."

Amos stared at the chief bell-ringer in blank amazement.

"Dr Austin asked you to ring the bells?" he asked incredulously. "Dr Austin? Are you sure?"

"Of course I'm bloody sure," Townsend spat out, the frustration of being seen as the bad guy who disrupted the big event of the day finally getting the better of him. "I'm so sorry, I'm terribly sorry," he gabbled all flustered. "I really didn't mean to say that. Especially in the House of God. May God forgive me," he added looking to the ceiling, which seemed at that moment to stretch back to the start of time, square upon square for the length of flat ceiling above the main body of the church then down into the arched chancel. "Please forgive me."

Amos was not sure if he or God was the intended recipient of this last plea but judged it best not to enquire. Instead, he spoke soothingly: "I quite understand, Mr Townsend, that this has been a very trying experience for everyone who was here at the time and that this must have been a terrible shock. But I do need to ask you when Dr Austin suggested the peal of bells and if she gave any reason why."

"It was three days ago. It was pretty short notice, I can tell you, to get 10 ringers together but some of the bell-ringers come from the fens where she has her practice and she is their GP so they were more conducive to the idea than they might have been. In any case, she stressed that the event would raise money for the church so we felt some obligation to cooperate. So, after a bit of arguing amongst ourselves, we agreed, although I have to admit that Dr Austin had to twist a couple of arms."

"She must have been pretty keen," Amos suggested.

"I suppose she must have been," Townsend conceded reluctantly. "It didn't seem that way, though. Anyway, we agreed to do it. It wasn't a problem for anyone. Dr Austin stressed that she wanted this event to put Boston Stump in its rightful place at the heart of the community. The idea was to make a joyful occasion of it."

"Joyful?" Amos asked thoughtfully. "Yet your choice of music – if that's the right word – was a little out of kilter if I may say so. *The Brides of Mavis Enderby* is a warning peal, is it not?"

"You're remarkably well informed," Townsend said enthusiastically. "Yes indeed, traditionally pealed from this very church to warn of East Coast floods or pirate raids. But few people would know that these days. I assumed that Dr Austin chose it because its curious name refers to a small Lincolnshire village."

Amos, however, did know all about the peal. He could not resist quoting triumphantly from Jean Ingelow's poem *High Tide on the Coast of Lincolnshire*:

"The old mayor climbed the belfry tower,

The ringers ran by two, by three;

'Pull if ye never pulled before;

Good ringers, pull your best,' quoth he,

'Play uppe, play uppe, O Boston Bells!

Play all your changes, all your swells,

Play uppe *The Brides of Enderby*'."

Townsend picked up his story: "For the past 40 years, since the last flooding of the East Coast in 1953, we have practised that peal once a month, always at low tide, as Dr Austin was well aware, so that no-one can mistake it for a genuine warning.

"We will ring it in earnest at high tide if the sea defences are ever breached again, heaven forbid."

"Did she not tell you when to start the peal?" Amos enquired. "Didn't she ask you to wait until the tower was empty?"

"She gave us a precise time to start," Townsend replied emphatically, "and we were spot on, at the lowest point of the tide, so no-one could mistake it for a genuine warning. The Haven was practically down to a dribble. Timing is everything for campanologists. She said that would be when there was a break between the experienced abseiling team members making the descent and the first of the volunteers. It would really attract attention, she said."

Amos resisted the temptation to ask "are you sure?" again, given the indignation he provoked the last time he queried Townsend's recollection of events.

"It didn't work out that way, though, did it?" he asked instead. "I gather that two people were at the top of the tower and another two, including Dr Austin, were on their way up when you started."

"How was I to know?" Townsend demanded. "I was in the belfry with the rest of my team. We did as we were asked and I resent taking the blame, though everybody seems to think it was my fault."

"I don't think anyone blames you for Simeon Knowles's death," the detective inspector reassured him. "You didn't get much chance to sabotage the equipment."

Chapter 7

A quick check with Detective Sergeants Swift from HQ and Burnside from Boston confirmed that all the key suspects had been interviewed and names and addresses of lesser mortals had been taken as far as possible.

The basic story from each suspect who had been interviewed in detail was much the same. Detective Inspector Paul Amos was satisfied that they now had a good idea of the morning's events up to the death of a man who was widely referred to as Saint Simeon.

The one person Amos did want to talk to again, Dr Lesley Austin, had disappeared. There had been no reason to detain her further once she had finished her interview. *Not to worry*, Amos thought, *we can catch up with her at her surgery in due course.*

"We need," Amos said, "to climb up to the walkway to see the spot where Saint Simeon got as near to God as he could before meeting his end. Gerry," he said to Burnside, "you don't have to come up if you don't want to. It'll be a long, steep climb."

"Like hell I won't come up," Burnside exclaimed irreverently. "I've worked directly opposite the Stump for years and never been to the top. Too mean to pay a couple of quid for the privilege. Now I can do it free. They say the views are spectacular."

The churchwarden came bustling up as the three officers made their way to the pillar at the northeast corner of the tower. The door at the bottom of the spiral stone stairway had stood open all the time with a lone policewoman on guard.

"It's a one way system," the churchwarden said. "You go up this tower and come down the other staircase. There's virtually nowhere to pass on the stairs. I trust that you are all in good health. No heart problems? There's 300 steps to the walkway."

Amos simply ignored the obsequious man and walked past him to the foot of the spiral stairway, nodding in acknowledgement to the sentinel policewoman.

"Go at a slow, steady pace," Amos said over his shoulder as he squeezed through the narrow doorway. Burnside followed him with alacrity but soon found that he was condemned to move at Amos's sensible speed. Swift tagged on the end with somewhat less enthusiasm.

They climbed the steep, circular stairway in silence, save for the rhythmic beat of footsteps and the increasing puffing emanating from Amos. At last the inspector reached a small alcove where he could pause for breath and allow Burnside to come bounding through.

"See you at the top," Burnside called back cheerily. "Last one up's a cissy."

It was a few moments before Swift reached Amos, by which time he had recovered his breath sufficiently to resume the climb. He set off again with scarcely a glance at Swift. His steady plod, plod, plod took him relentlessly higher and he became conscious in the confined space that the echo of Burnside's steps was slowing noticeably until it was beating at a lesser rate than his own footsteps.

Swift, in contrast, was not audible at any pace.

Amos eventually saw daylight percolating down through the gloom. He heard Burnside puffing his way onto the eastern walkway as he rounded the last twist of the tight, circular climb.

36

Burnside was collapsed over the railings atop the waist-high stone wall, desperately recovering his breath and trying to look nonchalantly across 250 feet of church roof to the river Witham meandering out to the nearest corner of the Wash.

"Fantastic view," he wheezed. "You can see all along the Norfolk coast to Hunstanton."

Amos had been all for walking straight along the north face of the tower to reach the western walkway from which Simeon Knowles had plunged to his fate but he succumbed to temptation and hoisted himself up the very steep step that separated him from the vision that had so captivated his Bostonian colleague.

Even without binoculars, you could just distinguish the big wheel at the fairground at Hunstanton.

"Best get on," Amos said, dragging himself reluctantly away from the vista. Burnside, having recovered his breath, nodded his assent. It was only then that they realised Swift was edging cautiously and nervously up the final steps of the narrow circular stairway.

She looked distinctly green. In the low light she had the appearance of a ghostly apparition approaching from the depths.

Chapter 8

Amos gasped.

"Juliet, what on earth has happened? Have you been attacked?" he asked urgently, flushed with guilt that in his quest to show up the bounding Burnside he had neglected his deputy.

Swift hovered at the exit to the stairway, committing herself to go neither left nor right, instead clinging to the central spine of the spiral.

"Sorry, sir," she gasped. "I'm not too good at heights. I thought I could do it."

"Go back to ground level," Amos urged her. "It's OK, there'll be no-one coming up."

"No, no. I've got to beat it. If I go back down to the next level and get my breath back I'll be all right."

With that, Swift edged gingerly back down the narrow spiral.

Amos hesitated for a moment but decided to plough on with his inspection. He and the now fully recovered Burnside walked along the north side of the Stump, admiring the view across flat land to the south wolds some 15 miles away. On the Western horizon, Lincoln Cathedral could be seen standing sentinel at the edge of the escarpment left by the retreating ice age.

Amos looked over the low wall down at the tent erected to cover the body of the unfortunate Knowles. The river had filled up and a couple of small boats that had been left high and dry when the abseiling event began were now bobbing merrily as water flowing from the sluice gates a hundred yards or so upriver met the incoming tide.

Ropes still festooned the outside Western wall of the Stump and a harness lay on the walkway. Two small fold-up seats were propped against the inner wall and a thermos flask lay on its side next to them as if it had been knocked over. A small plastic box stood nearby.

Amos prised the top off the box and looked inside. It contained sandwiches and two slices of madeira cake. The food had not been touched.

Burnside checked the ropes. They were in perfect condition and were fastened securely to metal rings set in the wall rising up to the lantern tower atop the Stump. Everything seemed to be in order.

Amos looked again down across the river. The sizeable crowd that had melted away as soon as police officers had started taking names and addresses was building up again and the appearance of two figures at what had been the point of no return for Simeon Knowles produced an extra attention.

"I don't think we can do anything more up here," Amos declared. "Let's make our way back down and see if Juliet is OK."

"I think we're supposed to come back down a different staircase," Burnside commented. "The one at this far corner." He indicated that they should go round the southwest corner and along the southern wall. "I don't suppose anyone will be coming up but you can hardly squeeze past, it's so tight."

The pair moved along in the direction that Burnside had pointed out, pausing momentarily to watch a two-carriage train from Skegness edge into Boston station before proceeding to Grantham.

The few seconds delay was sufficient to allow Swift to emerge at the corner behind and to call out to them. As they swung round in surprise, Swift began to edge gingerly towards them, her back firmly

39

against the inner wall of the walkway. She fixed her eyes on them, not daring to look up or down, or out across the stunning vista.

Burnside gallantly pushed past Amos and positioned himself between Swift and the low wall along the edge of the walkway. As he leaned back nonchalantly against the metal safety rail, Swift let out a screech and grabbed his arm, pulling him from the edge. An ironic cheer went up from the far river bank.

"Sorry," Burnside muttered. "I was trying to help."

"Don't," Swift replied ungraciously and, ignoring the hapless would-be Sir Galahad, sidled more quickly along to Amos.

At each corner there was a circular turret where the walkway passed through a small archway. Swift felt more comfortable in the enclosed space. Recovering her composure, she addressed Amos: "I went back down to the belfry level. I can usually climb higher if I go back a bit and take a few deep breaths.

"As I came down I heard someone coming up the stairs at a brisk pace and saw him open the door onto the floor the bell-ringers stood on. We'd walked past the door on the way up without really noticing it.

"So I followed him in. It was that creepy churchwarden. He seemed to be looking for something near the wall over to my left. He really jumped when he realised he was being watched."

Swift was all the time looking intently at Amos, not daring to let her eyes stray towards the wide open spaces beyond the archway.

"Did you see him actually pick anything up?" Amos asked.

"No, but he had his back to me so I can't be sure. He muttered something about checking if the bell ropes had been hung up properly and scooted off in a flash through a door in the corner nearest to him.

He'd gone before I could stop him and I could hear his feet clattering down the steps – there's another spiral stairway down that corner."

Amos nodded.

"Yes, there seems to be a one-way system. You come up one set of steps and go back down the other. Gerry. Get down those steps to the belfry. He may have come back."

Burnside squeezed with some difficulty past the other two officers, strode briskly along the south face and disappeared into the southeast turret.

"Ready for the final dash?" Amos asked in a kindly, fatherly way.

Swift nodded and walked unsteadily across to the sanctuary of the stairway without glancing over the bustling town laid out below in the sunshine.

Going down the roles were reversed. Swift scurried round and round the spiral, each step taking her closer to the safety of the ground while Amos stumbled, his eyes taking time to adjust from sunshine to semi-darkness and his larger feet finding the inside of the anticlockwise spiral too narrow for his left foot.

Amos finally arrived at the belfry level puffing more than he had on the ascent. Burnside was inquiring solicitously and persistently about how Swift was coping, much to her increasing irritation. She grabbed the opportunity to break away from the clearly disappointed Boston officer to report to Amos.

"Nothing here," she said in as business-like a tone as she could muster. "If the churchwarden was looking for something, either he had already picked it up when I saw him or he came back while we were at the top. Either way he certainly wasn't tidying up the bell ropes."

Amos looked around the small room. Sure enough, the ropes had been left higgledy piggledy as if dropped in haste.

"We'd obviously better have another word with him before he gets away," Amos said. "What's his name?"

The other two looked blank.

"Did either of you interview him?"

Again blank looks.

"He was never there when anyone was free to interview him," Burnside blustered. "He was always fussing around when you didn't want him. I'm not sure anyone got a statement from him. He kept slipping through the net."

There was no time to argue about whose fault it was.

"You two get down the stairs and find him," Amos ordered. "And don't let him go."

Juliet Swift swept to the door with a sideways glance to ensure that she would be through well clear of Burnside and set off down the stairs. Burnside followed with alacrity but a good couple of seconds behind.

Amos took one final look round the belfry room and followed them down the spiral stairway.

Chapter 9

Back down at ground level the church had cleared except for a dozen church officials who stood or sat around, looking blank and shocked. They were scattered in ones and twos as if not daring to speak to each other after the dreadful event. Some were in the open area between the north and south doors, others were in pews down the start of the aisle. All were silent.

Amos stood in the centre of the space at the base of the tower and looked round for the churchwarden. He was nowhere to be seen.

One of the young women who served in the shop on the north side of the open space, and who stood in its doorway with her colleague, guessed who the inspector was trying to locate.

"If you're looking for the churchwarden, he was here a couple of minutes ago," she proffered. "I saw him come down from the Stump but I didn't see where he went."

"He's like that tribe in Brazil, the invisibles," a nervous elderly lady in one of the pews chimed in. "You know," she added to her nearest companion, feeling the relief of just saying something, however unhelpful, "the one where they filmed the dam collapse in miniature on Ashby river. He just merges in and out of the woodwork, the same as the tribe did in the rainforest."

Sensing Amos's growing frustration, one of the bell-ringers stepped forward and said: "I saw him slip out through the north door. He moves like a shadow, a ghost."

Amos looked at the officer guarding the north door.

"Sorry, sir," he stammered. "I understood we were releasing people who had been interviewed."

Burnside took the sheets of interview statements and shuffled through them twice, shaking his head.

"It looks like he slipped through the net," he admitted warily, speaking as quietly as possible to minimise the broadcasting of the blunder.

"Let's start with his name," Amos said, with an air of barely controlled exasperation. He looked round in expectation but about half of those present had blank stares and for three or four seconds no-one spoke.

Then a general hubbub broke out. Some people were saying: "I don't know his name, do you?" Then the name Fred emanated from different directions. Something about "up the A16" emerged among the chatter.

Amos held up his hands for silence.

"For heaven's sake," he cried. "Someone must know his name and address."

The curate stepped forward.

"He was a very private man and hardly spoke to anyone unless he had to. When he had to give his name he usually just said Fred. His full name was Fred Worthington. But I don't know where he lived. He was very evasive about it."

"You didn't like to press him about it," another voice said. "You felt you were invading his privacy. He renders unto God the things that are God's when he is in church but his own life he renders unto himself."

Silence fell again. Amos rolled his eyes.

44

"He was churchwarden. You must have his address and phone number in the church records," he insisted.

No-one seemed to want to move, so great was the respect for the unbroken privacy of Fred Worthington, or perhaps it was the fear of his wrath.

Finally the vicar succumbed. He nodded to a middle aged man standing near the door to the tower stairway.

"Better get his details from the office, John, if you would," the vicar said quietly. "I think in the circumstances the needs of the investigating officers outweigh our desire to respect Fred's privacy."

As the official toddled off for the relevant details, Amos asked the general assembly: "I suppose it's too much to hope that anyone knows anything about him. Is he married? Children? Interests? Did he abseil?"

Amos, Swift and Burnside looked round, only to be met with headshakes and eyes turned towards the floor.

Uncomfortable minutes passed and Amos, without speaking, looked round the church officials and helpers one by one, then round again, and again, hoping someone would break ranks but without eliciting a response.

At last, the middle aged church official returned clutching a piece of paper which he handed without comment to the inspector. Amos glanced at the name, address and telephone number that it bore. He knew only roughly where the address was but declined to undergo the ignominy of trying to prise precise directions from the shell-shocked faithful.

"Has everyone here given statements and their addresses to a police officer?" he demanded

There was a general murmur but the inspector looked at each person in turn. This time their eyes met his and each individual either nodded or said "yes".

"I think we can let everyone go for now, thanks Gerry," Paul Amos told Burnside. Then to those non-police officers remaining he said clearly: "Please all make sure you are available over the next few days in case we need to speak to you again. Is anyone going away on business or holiday?"

A general murmur and shaking of heads indicated "no".

Burnside waved in his officers stationed at strategic points in the church, including the two officers who had respectively allowed Fred Worthington, the elusive churchwarden, to slip up the Stump and subsequently out of the north door.

The one from the bottom of the stairway up the tower protested once more that absolutely no-one except the three leading officers had got past him.

"Juliet and I will trace Worthington back to his home then we'll call it a day," Amos said to Burnside. "Are you on duty tomorrow, Gerry?"

"Not supposed to be," Burnside replied, "but of course …"

"No need, thanks," Amos cut him off. "We work enough unpaid overtime. Can you set us up an incident room in Boston police station and see that all the statements are available to us. We'll take it from there. See you Monday?"

"Yeah, sure," the sergeant confirmed. "See you Monday."

Amos ushered the police officers out of the south door like a shepherd releasing his flock from the pen. The religious asymmetry struck him. The shepherd was supposed to usher the flock in to safety,

46

the safety of the Stump that had protected mariners, farmers and traders from floods, pirate attacks and the pestilences of centuries. Now the Stump had been desecrated as the site of a great sin.

And here was Amos, removing the protectors of the material world while the guardians of the soul remained inside, lost and confused.

Amos and Swift returned to their car to find a parking ticket on the windscreen.

Chapter 10

Detective Sergeant Juliet Swift stepped smartly in front of Amos and peeled off the parking ticket.

"I'll deal with it, sir," she said firmly. Swift would pass it on to a junior officer on Monday to get it cancelled. She knew that Amos would have dealt with it himself.

Swift still had the car keys and Amos nodded to her to drive.

"A16, north," he said briefly. "About five or six miles. We'll ask directions from there. I'll put the siren on when we're well clear of the church. Worthington may grab some clothes and make a dash for it."

Finding the A16 was more tricky than the two officers, who were not familiar with Boston, expected. The pedestrian zone from the market place through to Wide Bargate forced them to pick their way through narrow back streets, then south down the right bank of another drain, until they reached the north east end of John Adams Way, the now grossly inadequate ring road that took traffic round the east and south of the town.

Five potentially precious minutes had been wasted before they were on the road that they actually wanted. They headed with lights flashing and siren wailing eastwards towards the roundabout where the A52 split off to the right along the coast to Skegness, thus halving the traffic.

Swift, on Amos's instruction, swung left following the Grimsby sign, past the Pilgrim Hospital and northwards.

Three miles on, the car shot with a series of jolts over the level crossing that marked the transit of the Boston to Skegness railway line, a lonely survivor of the savage ripping up of tracks in the county some 30 years previously in the 1960s. The route had been preserved at the behest of Billy Butlin and his holiday campers.

"Slow down and I'll switch the siren off," Amos told Swift. "We don't want to announce our arrival."

In Sibsey they stopped and asked directions that took them down the road signed for Sibsey Trader Mill, a windmill whose rotating sails now beckoned towards a tea room rather than sacks of flour.

"Next turning," Amos said abruptly, and in a side road off the side road they found the home of the elusive and shadowy churchwarden Fred Worthington. It was a short cul-de-sac with a circle at the end for turning. The houses on either side of the road were fairly modest but attractive, each with a short drive up to a garage. It looked to be a pleasant place to hide from the cares of the world.

"Pull onto the drive," Amos added, pointing to one of only two that were unoccupied. "Either he's not at home or he's one of the few people who put their car in the garage."

The former proved to be the case. There was no response to the very clear chime of church bells detonated by a press on the button on the front door. Nor was there any easy way of checking the back. Access down one side of the house was blocked by the garage reaching the border fence while the gate at the other side was locked.

"I could shin over," Swift offered.

"I wouldn't bother," Amos replied with a note of resignation as he peered in through the front window. "There's no sign of life and I've

49

no doubt the back door will be locked. If he's in and not answering the door he won't answer at the back either.

"Let's try the neighbours. We'll split and work round the close from opposite ends. Usual stuff. Has anyone seen him today? Has his car been in the drive in the past hour? Does he live alone? Any family? Anywhere he goes? Don't let on about what happened to Simeon Knowles. With a bit of luck they won't have heard about it yet. Just say it's routine and make out Worthington's not in any kind of trouble."

Worthington may have been out but his neighbours were very much at home. Information, however, was nearly as slow in coming as it had been at St Bartolph's.

The man had, apparently, lived in the close for best part of 20 years but didn't mix. There again, the same could be said of most of the neighbours, who either worked or did housework in the day and watched television at night as far as Amos and Swift could gather.

It emerged, though, that Fred Worthington had arrived with rather more sociable ideas. According to two neighbours whom Amos spoke to, back in 1977, soon after he moved in, he organised a street party for the Queen's Silver Jubilee.

Other residents had been reluctant but Worthington's enthusiasm had carried all before him and the event was a resounding success. Neighbour met neighbour and all resolved that "we must do this again".

However, attempts to make the party an annual shindig fell by the wayside and Worthington had gradually withdrawn into his shell, one shell among a row of shells occupied by hermit crabs.

It was Swift who stumbled on the one resident of the close who had, briefly, got genuinely close to Worthington. By now the two officers were only a couple of doors apart. She called Amos over.

"I think you should hear this, sir," she said. "This is Mr Johnson, Johnnie Johnson. I think he can help."

"You'd better come in," Johnson said amiably, adding unintentional irony: "We don't want the neighbours talking, do we."

Chapter 11

While the outside was distinctly traditional middle class conformism, the inside of Johnson's house was modern and minimalist. Nonetheless, it had been put together with coordination and an artistic eye.

At least there was no danger of relaxing into a comfortable arm chair and taking your mind off the investigation, Amos thought. He could see by the look on Swift's face that she thoroughly disapproved.

"You're asking about Fred, I gather," Johnson said. "Do you mind if I ask why?"

Amos sat up straight – it was admittedly difficult to do otherwise in the tubular steel and plastic chairs. Johnson was speaking as if Worthington were a real person rather than a shadow, as he had seemed to be at the parish church.

"There's been an incident at Boston Stump," Amos said simply. "We just need to ask Mr Worthington about the running of the church, as he is churchwarden there, and whether he witnessed anything. Unfortunately he had left before we had all the information we needed."

Juliet Swift coughed quietly to indicate that Amos was in danger of meandering too much. The inspector took the hint and asked: "Do I gather you are on familiar terms with Mr Worthington?"

"Mmm … well, I wouldn't go quite that far but I probably had more to do with him than anyone else in the close. I don't know if anyone told you, but in 1977 he organised a very successful street party for the Silver Jubilee. I don't think he'd been here all that long.

"Then he invited all the neighbours in for a glass of champagne on Christmas morning after he returned from the morning service at the Stump. This, too, went well the first year but one by one the neighbours dropped out for some reason or another. I was the last one to keep going so he held it in my favour. Not that we got off to a good start. I'm homosexual, inspector."

Johnson paused to gauge the reaction of the two officers.

Amos looked as relaxed as was possible on the uncompromising furniture. Swift, despite an effort at self control, bristled visibly and shifted in her seat. Johnson moved his gaze from the inspector to the sergeant.

"The church is nearly as bad as the police for its prejudice," Johnson continued with a distinct note of bitterness. "I thought with Fred living on his own he might be of a similar persuasion to me but when I touched his arm he pulled away and was quite cutting.

"Unlike most of your lot, though, Fred was willing to be reasonable. He was civil on the rare occasions we passed in the road and he recognised that I was the only one happy to exchange a few words. The other neighbours could hardly bring themselves to say hello to him.

"As they dropped out of the Christmas drinks they were too embarrassed to face him. And he held it heavily in my favour that I continued to support him. I never came onto him again and he slowly accepted me for who I am rather than a wretched sinner. It took an Act of Parliament to force the police to do the same."

Amos took a deep and audible breath, then continued as if the remark had never been spoken.

"You said that Mr Worthington lived alone. Perhaps he just wasn't good at personal relationships." Then the inspector added coldly: "Or perhaps he didn't fancy you as a sexual partner, just wanted you as a neighbour."

"You think if a man lives alone he must be gay?" Johnson retorted, overlooking the fact that he had made the same assumption several years ago. "As a matter of fact he wasn't. He was seeing some woman. She just didn't live here but she often stayed the night and she was here most weekends up to about a couple of years ago."

"Can you describe her?" Amos asked, a little more warmly.

Johnson leaned forward in his chair, his suspicions aroused.

"I'm a little reluctant to go into Fred's personal life behind his back. I thought this was just routine. Are you accusing him of something?"

"We need to know where he may have gone so we can contact him," Amos assured Johnson. "We may recognise the woman as someone at the Stump. Do you have a name for her?"

Johnson thought for a moment.

"Funnily enough, no," he replied. "I only ever met her properly on Christmas mornings. She called him Fred but he only ever referred to her as 'sweetheart' or 'darling'. Never by her name."

"Can you describe her?"

"About 5 foot eight, quite slim when she first visited as I recall but got a bit plumper by the end. Happens to all of us," Johnson added, patting his tummy.

He's relaxing again, Amos thought. *Don't put him on his guard.*

"I know what you mean," the inspector responded affably. "Can you remember anything else? Hair, for example."

"Short and dark, I think. I didn't really take much notice."

"And she stopped coming regularly, as far as you know, about a couple of years ago?"

"That's right. I don't think Fred will be with her. After she stopped parking on his drive, Fred started walking out some evenings and returning an hour or so later. I guessed he was going to the pub. There's one in the village. You could always try there.

"One evening I saw him setting off and I fancied a pint and a respite from my own company. Yes, I like pints," he said, shooting a hostile glance at Swift. "Not pina coladas." Then back to Amos: "As I guessed, Fred was there, sitting on his own on a bar stool. I'd given him time to get half way through his pint and he accepted my offer of another with a little hesitation. 'Don't worry, Fred,' I told him. 'I know you're spoken for.'

"'Not any more,' he said. And then he added something very strange that made me think she must have died. He told me: 'I'm only a churchwarden. She's left me for a saint'."

Chapter 12

Amos and Swift headed north, cutting slightly westward towards Simeon Knowles's home. They had the keys from his pocket with them, one of which would presumably give them access. There was no sign of anyone else at the house as they pulled up.

They got out of the car. Amos stood for a moment looking thoughtfully southwards across the great plain that was the fens. Flat land stretched before them, not only the 10 miles or more to Boston, where the Stump could be clearly seen, but also for a similar distance or more to the left and right.

The sun-facing south garden had been given over to vegetables rather than flowers, each section divided neatly by planks.

"Terracota rhubarb forcers," Swift said contemptuously. "How twee."

Swift rang the doorbell as a courtesy in case Knowles had someone waiting at home for him. After a few seconds' wait she quickly negotiated the two locks on the front door using the keys that had been found in the dead man's pockets.

"We'll look for a suicide note first," Amos announced. It was a sizeable house, so it took a few minutes to check round. No such missive was readily available and neither officer thought it likely that Knowles would kill himself so publicly yet hide away his reasons for doing so.

Next they concentrated on a room at the front of the house with views down towards the Norfolk coast at the far side of the Wash. It appeared to be some kind of library-cum-study, with books crammed into shelves round three walls.

A solid desk was arranged across the window with a swivel leather chair placed to maximise the benefits of the view. There was no computer but an old fashioned typewriter stood at one end of the desk as if pushed to one side until it was called back into use. A bottle of standard blue-black ink stood sentinel in the centre of the desk top at the back, with a fountain pen laid horizontally in front of it.

Amos opened the two long top drawers. One contained only typewriter paper, the other a typewriter ribbon still sealed in its package. The lower drawers were in two columns at either end of the desk, with a space between to accommodate the sitter's legs.

In the left hand side were receipted bills, the most recent on top. Telephone, electricity, gas, water and council tax were all mixed together according to date. The top drawer was half full but the two underneath were completely full.

"It looks as if Knowles paid each bill promptly as it came in, then put the bill into the drawer," Amos remarked as he studied the bank stamps on the top few. "As the top drawer filled up he presumably emptied the bottom drawer and moved the contents of the two higher drawers down one. The bills go back for six tax years."

The top right hand drawer contained monthly bank statements. In every case the transactions for an entire month fitted easily onto one short page. Amos looked again at the most recent utility receipts.

"He paid nearly all his bills in cash," the inspector said. "Yet he hardly ever drew cash out of the bank. He had his state pension paid monthly, plus a small private pension. That's about all that ever goes in. There are one or two large items such as holidays going out according to the itemised statement and very little else."

Amos pulled out the bottom right hand drawer. It contained income tax returns. Knowles declared his state and private pensions but nothing else. It was enough to tip him into paying some tax but not enough to warrant a higher tax band. *Just enough to keep the taxman off his back without being too onerous*, Amos thought.

Other than the one current account, there was no evidence in the desk of any other bank or savings account. Nor was there any cash.

"I suggest we search the house to see if there are any more financial documents, any cash, and any will," Amos told Swift.

They worked quickly and methodically through the large house but produced none of the items that Amos had listed. Nor was there anything else that seemed in any way relevant to the case.

As he glanced round, Amos noticed finger marks on the trapdoor leading up into the roof space. There was no ladder in sight so Amos grabbed a chair from one of the bedrooms and placed it on the landing under the trapdoor.

Although he was slightly short for a police officer, he could easily reach the ceiling and he gave the edge of the trapdoor a slight push. It sprung back and opened automatically. An expanding ladder was attached to the top side.

Amos pulled down the ladder and started to climb up into the darkness.

"Switch the landing light on please, Juliet," he requested. "It may just give me enough light."

She did so. By the time Amos was at the top of the ladder she was back with a bedside light with a beam that could be directed. She plugged it into a socket on the landing and passed it up to the inspector.

There was a pause as Amos looked round.

Finally he said: "This is where Knowles keeps his cash. Quite a bit of it, where it can't be seen. All stacked in £20, £10 and £5 piles."

Chapter 13

Amos was up at 7am next morning and was geared up for his "bowl of porridge for one" routine but Mrs Amos stirred as he got out of bed and that meant doing toast, which threw him.

His wife preferred toast and marmalade on Sunday just so that the day would be different, a habit she had got into because she had never been a churchgoer and her husband had worked as many Sundays as he had had off, so one day was pretty much the same as another.

Making toast for his wife and porridge for himself involved too much thinking so early in the morning. Should he have cereal? That difficult decision could be postponed.

So: empty half the kettle that Mrs Amos persisted in overfilling the night before; switch the kettle on; put two pieces of sliced bread into the toaster; put teabags into two beakers; put plate, butter and marmalade on tray.

Damn, the toast is ready too soon. Must have left too much water in the kettle. Quick decision, leave the toast in the toaster to keep warm. Now the kettle is boiling and the water can be poured into the beakers but the tea needs time to brew.

Grab two knives from the cutlery drawer and put them on the tray. Mrs Amos insists you cannot put the butter knife into the marmalade because that causes mould to form.

Her toast is now tepid but that solves one decision. Amos put the two pieces of toast onto his plate and put two fresh slices into the toaster. They would be ready by the time the tea had brewed, the teabags had been consigned to the waste bin and the milk had been added.

Amos took his wife's breakfast tray upstairs. Now there was another problem to resolve: when to have Sunday lunch. The Amoses preferred lunchtime on Sunday, or failing that as soon after 5pm as possible and no later than 7pm; otherwise on Monday or, in extremis, Tuesday.

But whenever they had it, it was always Sunday lunch: roast pork, beef, lamb or chicken in strict rotation with roast potatoes. Two hours notice was required. If Amos was home, he cooked it; if not, his wife did.

"Sunday lunch?" Mrs Amos inevitably asked as Amos handed her the breakfast tray.

"Definitely not lunchtime," Amos replied. "Tea time should be fine. Say six."

His wife grunted. "I'll make it seven. Ring me before five to let me know one way or another."

A second crisis over, Amos returned to his own breakfast. The toast was cold and he had forgotten to remove his own teabag, so the tea was stewed.

He could do without this hassle in the morning and now he realised that the butter was up in the bedroom. So was the marmalade. The apricot jam was taunting him from inside the open cupboard.

Amos slammed the toast and tea bag into the bin and poured muesli into his bowl. Bother, he had put the milk back into the fridge without thinking.

With a sigh, he settled down at the kitchen table with muesli and rebrewed tea. The Sunday newspaper had not yet arrived so there was nothing to read. What an exasperating start to the day. Amos hated his breakfast routine to go badly on a day when he was on duty.

Worse was to come when, as arranged, he picked up Detective Sergeant Swift from her home. Amos had driven to police headquarters at Nettleham just outside Lincoln and commandeered a marked police vehicle to avoid the ignominy of two parking tickets in successive days.

Jason, Swift's boyfriend, was in one of his maudlin, self-pitying strops. He stormed out to the car as Amos pulled up, the driver's side to the kerb.

"Juliet's supposed to be off duty today," Jason blurted out accusingly. "It's been arranged for ages. She worked yesterday. It's my cup match. Juliet promised she'd support me. It's my big chance."

"I can't help it, Jason," Amos said irritably. He usually talked Jason round with sympathy, the only method that seemed to work, but this morning Amos had neither the time nor inclination for delicacies. "Murders don't make allowances for the rugby season."

Swift was already opening the front passenger door.

"Get back inside, Jason, and pull yourself together," she snapped. "You know my work has to come first. You're not earning."

As Amos drove off hastily, he could see in the wing mirror the hapless Jason standing forlorn and tearful on the pavement watching the love of his life forsake him in his hour of need.

"Ah well," Amos said without conviction. "The day can only get better."

The rest of the morning, however, proved equally frustrating.

Chapter 14

"We'll go down the A15 to Sleaford and take the A17 into Boston," Amos said. "There's no point in calling in at Sibsey en route. Johnson, Fred Worthington's neighbour, rang HQ and left me a message.

"He had, as I asked him yesterday, given Worthington my phone number when he returned last night. Needless to say, Worthington didn't get in touch and Johnson suspected that he wouldn't from his attitude.

"Johnson heard a car starting up at about six this morning and he looked out of his bedroom window to see Worthington driving off. He rang to let us know."

Amos had, in fact, intended letting Swift, the faster driver, take the wheel in the hope of catching the elusive Fred Worthington at the Stump but swapping over would have meant prolonging the embarrassing altercation with Jason. In the event, the roads were pretty clear with not a tractor in sight so they reached Boston parish church by 10am in time to slip discretely into a pew furthest from the altar as morning service began.

The service was lightly attended.

"Looks like the faithful are not so keen that they get out of bed early in a Sunday morning," Swift muttered sardonically to Amos, who ignored her remark and continued to allow his gaze to wander around the congregation. Worthington was not readily visible.

Swift settled down in her seat for what was going to be, from her point of view, a boring hour. Her parents had not attended any church of any denomination, out of apathy rather than antagonism, and the whole rigmarole left her cold.

Amos stared passively at the ceiling through the opening prayers but to Swift's surprise he stood briskly as the introductory chords of the first hymn filled the vast chancel.

Swift remained seated sulkily, confident that she would not attract attention right at the back, although she glanced at Amos for any indication that she should comply with religious etiquette. The inspector, however, completely ignored her.

Despite having no hymn book, Amos joined in with gusto. To Swift's amazement, given that she knew Amos never went to church and was occasionally openly critical of organised religions of various kinds, the inspector knew all the words and the tune.

Swift cringed, glad that she had kept her head down. It was not that Amos sang out of key, it was that he sang in several different keys within the course of the hymn, sometimes sliding up or down a tone in mid-sentence, rather as the Beatles did in the middle of 'Strawberry Fields'.

Swift slowly lifted her head and looked down the nave. The sizable gaps between small groups of worshippers gave her ample opportunity to see if anyone flinched. The substantial choir, numbering in Swift's eyes as many as the congregation, were providing the bulk of the volume. Amos was filling in from the back. The feeble middle was swallowed up.

Swift leaned back again and closed her eyes. She tried to relax, as nothing could be done until this nonsense had run its course. Even the discomfort of the wooden pews could not offset her tiredness after a night of disrupted sleep following the guilt trip that Jason had put her through over missing the wretched rugby match. Time and again she half dozed off before some event or another rudely interrupted her somnolence.

Amos seemed to detach himself from the service, not kneeling for prayers, Swift noticed as she was stirred back to life by the shuffling of feet and rustling of bodies, or paying attention during the drone of the sermon, which brought her merciful relieve.

Then he was back with a vengeance each time the organ struck up, jolting her like an electric shock.

At last the service ended. Swift glanced at her watch. It was five to eleven, almost an hour wasted in a day when she was not supposed to be on duty and had things to do. Nor was there any sign of Fred Worthington, conspicuous once again by his absence.

Amos pushed past Swift as soon as the service concluded and was quickly up to the transept in search of his quarry before the congregation, such as it was, could start milling in the central aisle.

He spotted one of the church stalwarts who had been present on the ill-fated previous day. The man was evasive and unhelpful in shedding light on Worthington's movements that morning or his current whereabouts.

The vicar and choristers emerged from the vestry. They, too, showed no inclination to help.

Swift had held back and only after several unproductive minutes had passed did she realise that a woman standing by her right shoulder was Dr Lesley Austin. The GP had either come in after the service or she must have been sitting directly in front of the two police officers so that they had not recognised her from behind.

"Did you say you were looking for Fred Worthington?" Austin asked.

Swift was surprised, as she had not mentioned Worthington or indeed anyone else and Austin would have needed remarkably sharp hearing or good lip reading skills to hear Amos, who had spoken softly to minimise the fuss.

Before Swift could reply, however, Austin continued without waiting for confirmation: "Look for him at the Pilgrims' Memorial. He's obsessed with it."

Swift hastened to abstract Amos from the unhelpful throng a good 50 yards further up the nave. By now members of the congregation were standing talking in small groups in the aisle. As Swift reached the transept, she and Amos turned to see Austin sauntering casually out through the South door.

There were too many people milling around in the central aisle to catch her. Amos tried to push through but was thwarted by an influx of tourists arriving in a coachload, their entry timed to miss the morning service.

Then he spotted the young woman from the shop opening her door.

"Excuse me young lady," he said, in a stumbling fashion designed to give the impression of a helpless old man, a tactic that usually drew solicitous aid from any woman less than half his age. "Can you tell me where in the church I would find the Pilgrims' Memorial. I believe I will find Mr Worthington there."

The assistant chuckled.

"I'm afraid it's not in the church, sir," she replied. "It's at Fishtoft."

Then seeing the puzzled look on Amos's face, she explained in a kindly voice normally reserved for those of lesser intelligence: "The

66

memorial marks the spot at which the pilgrim fathers attempted to flee to Holland where they could get a ship to New England. They were arrested and imprisoned in Boston Guildhall before they escaped and eventually made it to America.

"It's on the North Bank of the channel that runs between the Wash to Boston port. They were trying to get far enough out of Boston so they could leave undetected. You can get through more directly from halfway round John Adams Way but it's a bit tricky. The easiest way to find it if you don't know the route is to follow the Skegness road and at Freiston turn right for Fishtoft. Then look out for the Pilgrims' Memorial sign."

Amos thanked the woman and looked for a last time round the church, which was emptying of worshippers and filling up with tourists, two small streams intermingling and swirling past without acknowledging each other.

It was too much to hope that Fred Worthington would be crawling out of the stonework that seemed capable of swallowing him like a ghost.

The inspector shrugged his shoulders with a sigh, turned to Swift and said: "Looks as good as anything. We really can't get much further forward until we speak to Worthington."

Swift nodded her agreement.

Following the directions to the memorial was easy but the road to what seemed like the middle of nowhere had more twists and turns than a convoluted detective story.

Unaware that the alternative route from near the port down along the bank of the Haven was much shorter, Amos remarked: "No wonder the pilgrims thought they could escape undetected from here."

67

Finally they found a rough piece of land at the roadside that passed for a parking spot. There was one car in it. Swift, who was driving, parked alongside it and the two police officers clambered up a steep bank that protected the land from high North Sea tides.

As they came over the top, they saw below them a lone figure sitting motionless on the grass at the water's edge and staring blankly at a small cargo ship manoeuvring gingerly down the narrow channel to the Wash.

Chapter 15

Fred Worthington failed to move a muscle as Amos and Swift bore down on him, although he must have been aware of their presence as they slithered down the rough path. As they came round him on either side, his gaze continued to follow the vessel.

"It must be good to just climb on board and leave everything behind. I wonder where it is going," he suddenly said in a flat, matter-of-fact tone.

"You don't seem surprised to see us," Amos said. "Yet you have gone to a great deal of trouble to avoid us."

"Just playing for time," Worthington replied wearily. "Just playing for time."

"Mr Worthington," Amos said with exasperation and only the minimum of courtesy. "We are conducting a murder inquiry which, with your church background, I would have thought that you would want to assist, not bring us on a wild goose chase round the fens."

"Quite so," Worthington replied absentmindedly, his gaze still on the retreating ship.

"Then will you kindly pay attention and account for your movements yesterday morning. When did you arrive at the Stump?"

"About eight. Give or take."

"And what did you do?"

"This and that. Just seeing everything was in order for the big event. Welcoming guests."

"Did you stay within the main body of the church? Did you go outside at all?"

"I was inside seeing that equipment wasn't left lying around for people to fall over. And making sure that visitors could get in without people blocking the doorway."

"Did you speak to anyone?"

"Lots of people."

"Such as?" The questions were becoming increasingly curt as Amos's patience boiled over.

"Lots of people," Worthington repeated, his eyes moving increasingly to the horizon as he followed the vessel that he wished he was on travelling to oblivion. "Church staff. The woman from the bookshop. Tourists. The abseiling club."

"Did you speak to Simeon Knowles? Or Dr Austin?"

"Yes, and yes," came the world-weary reply.

"Did you see anyone tamper with Knowles's harness at any point before he went up the tower? Or anyone with a knife before or after?"

"No and no," Worthington said hastily but firmly. His eyes moved momentarily to the ground as he emitted his answer, then they returned to the disappearing cargo ship.

"Look at me," Amos commanded. Worthington slowly complied.

"Why did you go up to the bell-ringers' room?"

"Just seeing that everything was OK," Worthington replied simply. "I was in a state of shock."

"You were looking for something," Amos went on, ignoring the feeble excuse. "What?"

Worthington shook his head but uttered no sound. His gaze met Amos's stare, then he turned seawards again to observe the now empty horizon.

"I can see we're going to get nowhere," Amos stated the obvious. "I gave you every chance to cooperate. If you won't tell us what you removed from the Stump, perhaps we'll find it at your house. I'll get a search warrant."

Amos hated tearing other people's homes apart, even when they were guilty. It was an invasion of their privacy almost as obscene as a burglar breaking in and turning the place over. The intrusion was all the more offensive when he knew he was highly unlikely to find anything that would incriminate the hapless churchwarden.

It was therefore something of a relief when Worthington rose slowly to his feet and looked at Amos properly for the first time before saying: "No need. You can look for what you want. You won't find anything."

I'm sure he's right, Amos thought to himself, *but I'm going to put him through it after the way he's messed us around.*

"Very well," the inspector said sarcastically. "We'll take up your gracious offer. Detective Sergeant Swift will accompany you in your car back to your house…" Then seeing the look of horror on Swift's face, he swiftly corrected himself: "Better still, I will ride in your car and my sergeant will follow in the police car."

The three of them made their way back over the banking and down to the makeshift car park. Only now did it strike Amos how vulnerable this part of the county was, so flat and with so much of it below river level.

71

Swift almost snatched the police car keys from Amos and got into the driving seat quickly. Amos casually pulled open the passenger door as Worthington released the lock.

"Do you want me to drive," Amos offered. "You seem preoccupied. Are you sure you're up to it?"

"Of course I can drive my own car," Worthington snapped.

Amos did not want to alienate him in case he withdrew his offer to let the officers search his house. However little they found of value affecting the investigation directly, it would at least give them an insight into this reclusive and mysterious man.

As they left the historic site, Worthington surprised Amos by swinging right rather than left back along the way towards Boston that Amos and Swift had used.

"Don't worry, I know what I'm doing," Worthington remarked dryly.

The churchwarden cut across the A52 and drove along narrow back roads. Although they were all properly surfaced they were for the most part too narrow for even a couple of cars to pass by without slowing to a crawl. For about three miles the road was dead straight with a deep water-filled drain uncomfortably placed at Amos's side.

As it happened, they did not encounter another vehicle, despite Worthington extending the length of time taken by carefully ensuring that Swift was not left behind.

Finally they came out onto the A16 and a few minutes later Worthington pulled onto his drive with Swift parking across the end of it.

The house was immaculate except that an airer was parked in the middle of the kitchen bearing a complete set of clothing including jacket and trousers. Swift touched them. They were still damp.

"You were keen to get the clothes you were wearing yesterday washed," she remarked casually without so much as a glance at Worthington. The items could have been any day's clothing but it was a reasonable assumption.

"Cleanliness is next to godliness," Worthington replied simply.

"What was on them? Blood?"

"Don't be ridiculous," Worthington snapped. "Simeon Knowles wasn't stabbed. Or was he?"

"We won't know the cause of death until the post mortem," Amos interrupted sharply. Then to Swift, he said: "Let's have a look round."

"I'll come round with you," Worthington interjected. "I don't want anything planted."

"Suit yourself," Amos replied with bad grace.

He wandered round the living room, aimlessly opening drawers. Worthington watched him nonchalantly while Swift stood still, unsure what to do.

Eventually Amos led the way into the hall, followed by Worthington with Swift carefully bringing up the rear so she could keep Worthington in sight.

Amos pulled out a drawer in an occasional table where the telephone stood. He extracted an address book and flicked through it. Worthington had an annoying habit of listing some numbers by surname and some by first name, so that, for example, the page for L included an entry for Jim Lawrence and two for Lesley, one marked home and one labelled surgery. A few names also had addresses and some didn't. It was a contrast to the otherwise apparently orderly and methodical life of the churchwarden.

"You know Dr Austin?" Amos asked.

"She was my doctor," Worthington replied. "When I lived down in the fens," he added quickly.

Wasn't this all the fens, Swift wondered, *or were there different levels of fens? Did people in Sibsey look down on the sons of the soil?*

Amos, however, quickly persisted: "You list your doctor by her first name, do you?"

Worthington shrugged his shoulders and made no reply.

"I'd like to keep this book if I may," Amos said suddenly. "I'll let you have it back in a couple of days."

Worthington gave another silent shrug.

"Let's go," Amos said to Swift, then he added to Worthington: "Thank you for your cooperation. We'll be in touch."

Another shrug was again Worthington's only response. He looked relieved to be getting rid of the intruders. Swift was torn between wanting to put a door between herself and this creep and giving the place a proper going over.

As Worthington closed his front door behind them, Swift spoke with vituperation: "Why are we letting him get away with it? He's obviously covering something up. We need to find out what he recovered from the Stump."

Amos was taken aback. Swift rarely gave a display of insubordination. Worthington had really got to her.

"I don't believe for one moment that we would have found anything in his house. Whatever he had – and it was presumably a very sharp blade – is probably in the river. Dislike of a suspect is no justification for searching his house.

"Let's get in the car and see who's in his phone book."

Swift still had the car keys and Amos moved to the passenger side. With his back to the house he flicked through the address book, keeping it out of sight of the lounge window.

As Swift walked round to the driver's side, Amos said suddenly: "Do you think you could find your way back along the route we came on?"

"I can remember a bit of it," Swift said. "We came onto the A16 alongside the bowls club so we can find our way as far as that but I'm not sure I could do the full route."

"You won't need to," Amos assured her. "Just get us across the A16. I recognise the name of Hollyoaks farm in the address book. I noticed the sign as we drove past just a few minutes before we came out onto the A16. Let's see if we can find it."

Swift did indeed manage to pick up the route in reverse, at least to the point where Amos shouted out excitedly: "There it is!"

Chapter 16

Swift pulled into the farmyard, which mercifully sported more clinker than cow pats, and they knocked on the farmhouse door. A middle aged woman, chubby and glowing with health, answered.

"Mrs Mason, I presume," Amos said smoothly. "Please don't be alarmed but we are police officers," he added, reaching for his warrant card.

Mrs Mason cut him short.

"I take it this is about poor Simeon. We heard on the farmers' grapevine. You'd better come in."

They were shown into a kitchen where Mrs Mason was busy baking.

"It *is* about Simeon, I take it," she repeated.

Amos nodded. He decided not to mention that this address had been picked out at random from Fred Worthington's book because it just happened to be within easy reach.

"That man was a saint," Mrs Mason said fervently. "If there's anything we can do to help, you've only to ask."

"How did you come to know him?" Swift interjected impatiently. She was standing near the oven, while Amos had seated himself at the kitchen table.

Mrs Mason paused from rolling pastry and leaned forward, looking nervously from one officer to the other. She put down the rolling pin, went to the door to look across the yard, then returned to the table.

"Please promise me you won't let my husband know I told you," she said, then hesitated.

Amos smiled and nodded, then squeezed her hand resting on the table when he realised that the woman was close to tears.

"Steve – my husband – won't have it mentioned, he was so ashamed, but I think Simeon should have the credit he deserves. We were desperate. Steve was getting suicidal. It was a bad year on the farm. We lost half the harvest because of the weather. Simeon bailed us out.

"It took ages to pay him back but we worked hard, pulled together and we're still here to tell the tale. We owe everything to Simeon. He was so patient, waiting for his money. He used to call round once a week just to make sure we were all right."

"Do you mind if I ask you how much he lent you?" Amos asked sympathetically, maintaining his gentle hold of the woman's hand.

"I don't rightly know," Mrs Mason said. "Steve takes care of the finance and the paperwork. Not that he's done any training for it. You won't ask him, will you?" she asked urgently, withdrawing her hand. "He'll know I told you."

"No, no," Amos replied soothingly. "No need. But did you approach Mr Knowles or did he approach you?"

"It was Mr Worthington at St Botolph's who introduced us. Mr Worthington said Simeon had helped several farmers in distress. He said it would all be done very discreetly and no-one else would ever know.

"It was never mentioned at the farmers' meetings but we do know that one farmer got into serious trouble. Poor soul, he killed himself. Even Simeon's money and sweet nature couldn't save him. There's a high suicide rate among Lincolnshire farmers, you know. Simeon's the only one who seems to care round here."

Chapter 17

"Let's go back to Boston police station," Amos said dispiritedly as he and Swift climbed into the police car.

"We'll have a look through the witness statements to see if there's any clue why someone would want to murder a man who was so universally loved. We'll make sure everything is set up and we can assemble a team tomorrow. I think Sunday lunch will be eaten early tonight."

Amos was surprised to see Detective Sergeant Gerry Burnside waiting patiently at Boston police station as they entered the building.

"Hello, Gerry," the inspector called out. "I thought you were off duty today."

"Thought I'd just see that everything was in order in the incident room," Burnside replied cheerfully, casting a glance at Swift as he did so. "Can't have County HQ thinking we country hicks can't hack it."

Burnside waved the two visitors down a corridor towards an open door, gallantly standing back to allow Swift through first, but she stood back, saying curtly: "You lead the way. You know where we're going."

Burnside complied reluctantly.

The room was immaculate. Amos had never seen an incident room so clean, so devoid of rubbish and with tables and chairs so carefully laid out. Two notice boards with pins had been set up plus a whiteboard with assorted coloured markers.

On the tables, witness statements had been laid out with military precision, as if someone had used a ruler to line them up. The piles of files were labelled 'Abseilers', 'Church officials', 'In church', 'Outside church' and 'Across river'.

"I'm afraid the phones won't be connected up until tomorrow morning," Burnside admitted sheepishly.

"Thanks, Gerry, you've done us proud," Amos remarked. Burnside, however, was paying more attention to Swift than to Amos and kept edging as close to her as possible despite her attempts to put at least one desk between them.

Finally Amos cottoned on to his deputy's discomfort. Normally Swift was no nonsense in discouraging unwanted advances, from colleague or criminals alike.

"I'm sure everything is in order, Gerry," the inspector said. "Juliet and I will just go through the statements for a full picture. I'll get the autopsy details tomorrow morning, though I don't suppose there's much doubt about the cause of death. Can you spare us a couple of detective constables from tomorrow onwards?

"I don't think there's any point in tying up two sergeants and I'm used to working with Juliet. Besides, the Chief Constable is interested in this case so you're better off out of it."

Burnside, however, looked rather disappointed and showed no inclination to go home to his wife and family.

"I've been through all the statements of people in the church at the time," he said.

"Tell you what, Gerry, as you're here," Amos said, "why don't you sit here and go through the statements of those across the river? There aren't so many of those and you can let us know if they throw up anything different from the statements you've already read."

Burnside took up the invitation readily and sat down where Amos had indicated with the relevant small pile in front of him. Swift looked distinctly disgruntled but as soon as Burnside was seated Amos sat next to him behind the largest pile marked 'In church' and moved the 'Outside church' dossier over to his other side, disrupting the unnaturally orderly layout of documents. He nodded to Swift to check this pile, thus putting his body between the two sergeants.

The three read in silence. Burnside and Swift finished at roughly the same time and Amos swapped their piles over. The two sergeants had completed their second allotments by the time Amos had finished his larger set.

"Let's compare notes," Amos said. "Quite a number of people were near to or actually spoke to Simeon Knowles as he waited to go back up the tower. With the melee and pushing and shoving, many of them were close enough to tamper with the harness unnoticed.

"Of those we can account for, Dr Austin had the best opportunity as she was close to Knowles for much, though not by any means all, of the time they were in the body of the church. She also went up the tower with Knowles and was with him at the top.

"The two abseiling officials ditto. Fred Worthington had opportunity at ground level. The chief bell-ringer just possibly, although he denied getting really close to Knowles and too many eyes were upon him in the short time he was down below.

"We have half a dozen members of the public who gave statements. Four were visitors from outside the area with no apparent connection to Knowles. The other two were a local farmer and his wife who say they just came along to give support. They were seen talking animatedly to Knowles while Austin and Worthington were arguing with the chief bell-ringer, so we have to count them in as possibles.

"Of the people who were seen, but are not accounted for, are a family of American tourists who seemed very interested in tracing their ancestry, and a woman aged about 30 with a small child who were probably also tourists - we don't know where from as no-one seems to have spoken to them. Does that sum things up fairly? Have I missed out any reasonable suspects?"

The two sergeants indicated their agreement.

"You've both read the statements of the people outside the church, such as we were able to corner," Amos resumed. "Do either of you see anything in any way significant or that adds to the sum of our knowledge?"

This was greeted with the shaking of heads.

Amos looked at his watch. It was still not 4pm but there was a drive back to Lincoln for himself and Swift, not to mention Sunday lunch to be taken before 7pm.

To get Burnside well away from Swift, Amos wrote down a number on a piece of paper and handed it to the Boston sergeant.

"Do me a favour, would you please, Gerry," he said, "and ring my wife. Tell her Sunday lunch at 6pm. Don't ask," he added quickly as Burnside opened his mouth to query this odd timing. "Sunday lunch is Sunday lunch."

Chapter 18

Burnside wandered down the corridor none the wiser but he returned almost immediately.

"American tourist to see you," Burnside announced peremptorily as he ambled back into the incident room. "Don't forget to tell him this is the real Boston. Some of them think it's in Massachusetts."

As Amos rose to his feet, Burnside added: "He's brought his holiday snaps with him. Have fun."

Amos was halfway down the corridor to the front desk when he heard Swift say acidly: "How's your wife today, sergeant? Still living?"

The American introduced himself as Bobby Franklin. His accent was mercifully mid-Atlantic rather than a drawl.

"I've just read in the morning newspaper about the dreadful incident in Boston church. Are you the officer in charge?"

Amos nodded. He hadn't had chance to check if the story had made it into the nationals. Apparently it had done.

"I was in the church yesterday morning. My ancestors were from Lincolnshire and I've always wanted to visit but I've never got out of London on my business trips. My wife's descended from one of your poets. It's all there in the church."

"I believe you have some photographs," Amos butted in, anxious to avoid two full family histories.

"Yes, sorry," Franklin said apologetically. "I finished a roll of film and had the snaps developed at the express photo shop in Boston town centre in the afternoon. When I saw the news this morning I thought I'd better bring them in, in case they are of any help."

"That's very considerate of you, Mr Franklin," Amos said gratefully. "Please come through to the incident room."

As they walked down the corridor, Amos asked: "Did the police take a statement from you yesterday?"

"No, we'd left before it all happened. My kids were furious they missed out on all the excitement. But I think I saw the guy who died before he went up the Stump. He's on one of my pics."

Amos laid the photographs out on a spare table. He and Swift studied them carefully. Most were general photographs of the exterior and interior of St Botolph's. Franklin had naturally posed his family for some shots but other unconnected people inevitably found their way into the fringes of several frames.

"Here," Amos exclaimed. "The woman with the boy."

The exterior photograph showed them in the background entering the South door.

"Or is the boy with this other woman?" Swift suggested, pointing to an interior shot. "They could be together and there's no sign of the woman in the first pic. Both women are about the same age and right for the mother of a six-year-old. And what about the two middle-aged men," Swift went on, referring to another interior scene. "I don't remember seeing them when we arrived and I had a good look at all the faces of people still hanging around inside the church. They must have been very close to where Knowles was sitting while the brouhaha was on."

A man and a woman, both aged about the mid-40s and smiling broadly, seemed to be speaking to Knowles in another photograph.

Knowles had his arms stretched out towards them as if he wanted to embrace them.

"You're welcome to keep any pictures you want," Franklin said. "I've still got the negatives. I can soon get reprints done."

"I'm sorry, Mr Franklin, but I shall need the negatives. We may need to print more copies, do blow-ups and they could be evidence. I can let you keep most of the prints. I just need three or four. I wouldn't ask if it wasn't vital.

"Let me have your movements in the UK and your address in the US and I'll send you a set of prints to replace the ones we are keeping. I'll let you have the negatives in due course if I possibly can."

"Hey, that's all right," Franklin replied magnanimously. "Glad to help. The kids'll be thrilled to bits we're helping with a homicide. We're leaving Boston as soon as I've finished here. We've done all the Pilgrim Fathers history. We're staying at the White Hart in Lincoln for a couple of nights before moving on to York."

Franklin wrote down his address in Boston Massachusetts and handed it to Amos.

The inspector picked out six photographs and extracted all the negatives from the packet that Franklin had placed on the table. He handed back the rest of the prints to their owner.

"Thank you," Amos said. "Detective Sergeant Swift will show you out and you can resume your holiday."

Chapter 19

"I must go and find a phone," Amos said, leaving the bemused American staring at a bank of telephones laid out on the tables but dead to the world.

Burnside had already left, no doubt having forgotten to ring Mrs Amos, which was just as well as the inspector would now be seriously delayed for Sunday lunch, even at 6pm.

Amos rang HQ at Nettleham. David, the Chief Inspector's fussy press officer, would not be around on a Sunday afternoon and could be bypassed.

"Get *BBC Look North* and the *Evening Echo* in for an emergency press conference in an hour's time, or as soon after as they can make it," he ordered the detective who picked up the phone. "We need a camera crew from *Look North*. Tell them it will be worth it. Just get them."

Amos slammed the phone down before the detective could protest.

"Get the car moving," he ordered Swift as she returned from seeing Bobby Franklin off the premises. "I'll grab our stuff from the incident room."

There was not, in fact, anything to grab apart from the precious photographs. Swift had brought the car from the car park round to the front door in the sixty seconds it took for Amos to emerge and they were soon picking their path through the traffic on John Adams Way with siren blaring and lights flashing.

Eventually they picked up the Sleaford signs and followed the A17 until they swung north along the A15 towards Lincoln.

Luck was still running for Amos. A TV camera crew was making its way back from Grantham to Hull and was diverted to Nettleham, while an *Evening Echo* reporter had also been despatched to find out what Amos was so excited about.

Amos addressed the assembly of two reporters and a cameraman in his office.

"This is all on the record," he announced. "You can start filming.

"I have here some photographs taken in Boston Stump just before the tragic accident that occurred yesterday morning when a man taking part in an abseiling charity event fell to his death. I must stress that all the people appearing in these photographs were present legitimately and none of them are under suspicion. They were photographed entirely by chance.

"I am appealing to anyone pictured here who has not yet made a statement to the police to contact my team at Boston Police Station urgently. You may have vital information.

"Also, if you recognise anyone, will you please ring me and give me their names. You will NOT be getting anyone into trouble. I repeat, they are not suspects and they left the church entirely legitimately, possibly well before the accident occurred. If nothing else, we need to eliminate them from our inquiries."

Amos paused for breath. How he hated that last phrase, which was always a lie, like 'your cheque is in the post' or 'of course I'll still love you in the morning'. The truth was that all these people were possible suspects and he hoped one of them was indeed the murderer and could be promptly arrested as such.

The reality, alas, was that they almost certainly would be eliminated and the phrase would turn out to be the truth after all.

The TV reporter took back his microphone.

"Can we assume that this is a murder inquiry?" he asked, before putting the microphone back under Amos's nose.

"At this stage we are treating the death as suspicious," Amos answered coolly, unsure whether the adjective murder would cause people to shy away or hasten forward. "We shall know more after the post mortem is held tomorrow and we have had the opportunity to question more witnesses."

"But you can't rule out murder?"

"No, we can't rule out murder. But the important thing at this stage is for anyone who was at Boston church yesterday morning to come forward."

There were no further questions.

"Can you film the photographs on the table as close up as possible?" Amos asked the cameraman. "Then I can give the prints to the *Evening Echo*. I'll tell you the people I am particularly keen to identify. Is there any way you can circle them for public consumption?"

All three media people nodded. Amos picked out the boy and the two women who could have been his mother, the man and woman smiling at Knowles, plus a couple of men.

"Please say that Detective Inspector Paul Amos is in charge of the inquiry, assisted by Detective Sergeant Juliet Swift, but that anyone at Boston Police station will take down details if we are not available."

Once the filming was over, camera crew, *Evening Echo* reporter, Amos and Swift made their escapes. Amos glanced at his watch. He'd promised to ring home to say when he'd be back but it was a bit late now for his wife to put the chicken in the oven. Better to get Swift back to Jason then himself home and they could both get the retribution over with.

Chapter 20

Amos drove Swift home feeling rather pleased with how the day had improved from unpromising beginnings. Doing a TV slot always made him feel slightly smug, especially when it could be slipped out without Chief Constable Sir Robert Fletcher or his obsequious press officer David having the chance to interfere.

No doubt there would be hell to play the next day but Amos had the excuse that Fletcher had specifically wanted to get this investigation moving. Rather more discreetly, perhaps, but moving.

However, Amos found that the day was starting to come full circle as he pulled into the road where Swift lived. He immediately spotted Jason, her lachrymose, rugby-playing boyfriend, sitting forlornly on the garden wall. He was still wearing his dirty rugby kit.

Jason was just staring blankly at the pavement. He hardly glanced up as the car pulled to a halt alongside him.

Swift, visibly alarmed, jumped out before the vehicle was fully stationary.

"Jason, are you all right?" she asked, urgently but gently.

Jason's response was to launch into uncontrollable sobs.

"I got sent off. I lost my rag and hit someone," he gasped between sobs. "We lost. We're out of the cup. It's all my fault."

"Oh Jason, I'm so sorry," Swift said tenderly, embracing his huddled form. "I should have been there for you. I'm so sorry."

She helped him down from the wall, picked up the holdall containing his clothes that lay on the pavement and supported him up the short path to the house without a backward glance at Amos. The inspector heaved a sigh and drove off, hoping against hope that his own homecoming would be less stressful. He swung hastily across the road without a glance in his mirror, anxious to avert his eyes from the tragi-comedy that had unfolded on the pavement.

The blast of a car's horn narrowly averted a nasty collision, forcing Amos to swing sharply to his right. A quick look down the pavement showed that Swift and Jason were already through their front door and had thus missed the inspector's ignominy.

Amos was soon feeling buoyed again by the thought that tonight he would be on *Look North* and he hurried home in eager anticipation.

There was an ominous silence as he opened the front door. No cheery welcome nor blare of television.

The door of the dining room was wide open, which was unusual. Amos walked down the passageway gingerly, a sense of impending disaster growing with each step.

There on the dining table was the fully cooked chicken with two slices carved from its breast, vegetable tureens, a half full gravy boat and one plate, knife and fork. Dinner had been cooked, consumed and left to go cold.

In the front room, Mrs Amos was sitting in icy silence, her arms folded.

Their eyes met. Amos knew better than to speak.

Finally, Mrs Amos said: "Gerry Burnside rang. You told him you'd be home for dinner. It's on the table. I've had mine."

With that, she got to her feet, pushed past her husband and stomped upstairs.

So Gerry had rung after all. With a sigh, Amos slouched into the dining room. His appetite had waned and he ate little. Then he poured a scotch and went through into the front room to watch the television in glum, solitary silence.

There was nothing on the regional news after all. His interview had been held over until Monday.

Amos switched off the TV and trudged up to bed. Mrs Amos was in the spare room.

Chapter 21

The sense of impending doom that had enveloped Amos at home on the previous evening returned long before he made his way to the mortuary the following morning.

It was no use taking breakfast to Mrs Amos when she was in this mood and the breakfast for one routine that Amos had perfected for those mornings when his wife was still asleep was too much to think about.

So juggling the boiling of porridge and kettle was abandoned in favour of toast, which was normally reserved for off-duty Sundays. Amos hated this breaking of routine.

It would, as Amos thought from time to time, be so much easier if he lived on his own with his irregular working hours. It was not as if he and his wife were particularly close any more. However, when the possibility of a split arose he always backed away from the lurch into the unknown.

In contrast, pathologist Brian Slater was in one of his cheery moods. You could tell, Amos knew, that he was in a good mood because he was attempting to whistle the hymn *Take it to the Lord in prayer*. The effort was more wind than whistle but was just about recognisable.

The hymn had irritated Amos in his Baptist churchgoing days and he suspected that Slater whistled or, more accurately, blew it just to be annoying. Taking your troubles to the Lord, in prayer or by other means, seemed particularly ineffective to Amos when his burdens were generally imposed by a chief constable who was reluctant to ease them.

"Trade's good," Slater announced blithely as he glanced up from the slab when he heard Amos enter the mortuary. "Bit too good if anything."

"When's Simeon Knowles scheduled for?" Amos asked.

"This year, next year, sometime, never," Slater replied with a sigh that indicated that Amos was in serious danger of dispelling the pathologist's unusual air of contentment. "Who knows? I'm sure I don't."

Having wheezed through a line and a half of his hymn, Slater went back to the beginning and started again, a habit that particularly infuriated Amos, who felt that if the discordant imposition had to be endured it was better to get it over and done with.

"For goodness sake, Brian, shut up that infernal racket," Amos exploded. "When are you doing the autopsy on Simeon Knowles? It's a simple enough question."

Slater stopped again mid line but the twinkle was back in his eye.

"Bit narky, today, inspector," he said after a pause.

"It's no use taking it out on me," Slater added, breaking off from his attentions to the half carved up body lying before him and looking Amos in the eye.

"Sir Robert Fletcher, the Chief Constable himself, has so decreed," he went on grandly, "we have two drug overdose victims to prioritise. The latest campaign, you know."

Amos knew only too well. The Chief Constable frequently launched a new crusade, running them for a few months with great intensity at

94

the expense of other police work, then tiring of them and moving on to a new hobby horse.

Drug abuse among the young was the latest thing. Fletcher's crusades were at their most intense as he built up to the next quarterly meeting of the East Midlands chief constables, now looming large in Lincoln. At this stage in proceedings, all other aspects of justice took a back seat and Fletcher was always particularly edgy when he was acting as host.

"I'm afraid you're low priority," Slater confirmed. "Low priority."

"Low priority?" Amos exploded again. "It's a murder, for heaven's sake."

"Only a murder," Slater commented with a shrug of his shoulders. "Only a murder. You already know what he died of so what's your problem?" The pathologist indicated by raising his arm and making a diving motion with his hand: "Splat! You don't need me to tell you. I can tell you he played a mean clarinet, though. Terrific. Funnily enough, he hated jazz but he came round the villages and accompanied carol singing every Christmas without fail. "

Take it to the Lord in prayer started up again from the beginning but Slater interrupted himself after only four puffs.

"Why don't you take it up with the Chief Constable?" he suggested genially. "If he gives the go-ahead, I can slot you in first thing tomorrow. Best I can offer – and only if Fletcher says so."

Amos was reluctant to go to the Chief Constable. It was hard to get any sense out of him when he was in full flood with a new campaign plus he knew Knowles personally; the inquiry had not got very far yet; and Slater was right to say that there was really no doubt as to how Knowles had died.

Slater broke off from another tuneless attempt at his favourite hymn.

"I think Sir Robert has lost interest in this case," he remarked casually. "Perhaps there are things he doesn't want coming out. Why do you think he put you on it?" Seeing Amos look startled and hurt by this observation, Slater went on: "Why don't you go and see Dr Austin? She can tell you anything else you want to know about Knowles."

Amos, who was pondering the distinct possibility that Slater could be right about Fletcher, looked at the pathologist quizzically.

"Didn't you know?" Slater asked with a look of amusement. "She was his doctor. He consulted her often enough."

Chapter 22

Detective Inspector Amos stomped back to CID in an even worse mood than when he had left it a quarter of an hour previously.

He called Juliet Swift into his office curtly. Swift feared the worst. Amos rarely hid away in his office, a small room that he had neither sought nor asked for, preferring to work with his team rather than setting himself apart. The Chief Constable had bestowed it upon him in a rash moment as a reward for a piece of crime solving.

Swift closed the door behind her. Amos was staring out of the window in silence.

"What is it, Sir?" the detective sergeant asked. "You're obviously not best pleased."

Amos turned round with an air of resignation.

"It's OK, Juliet. It's nothing you or the team have done."

He took a deep breath.

"We don't have the post mortem on Knowles and I don't know when we are going to get it. I daren't go to the Chief Constable to try to get it prioritised because he's all wrapped up in his wretched anti-drugs campaign. He'll only complain if I do and you know as well as I do that the longer he is kept out of this inquiry the better.

"However, what has really got up my nose is that it turns out that Lesley Austin is Simeon Knowles's doctor, for heaven's sake. Why the hell didn't she mention it? Please don't remind me," he said holding up his hands. "I know. I interviewed her myself. It never occurred to me to ask because I assumed she would have mentioned it. Why on earth did she say nothing?"

"Perhaps she didn't think it was relevant," Swift suggested. "After all, his medical history had no bearing on his death. It's not as if he had a heart attack at the top of the Stump and toppled off."

"Well, we'll soon find out," Amos said decisively. "You and I will pay Dr Austin a visit. And while we're there, watch for any indications that she and Knowles were having an affair. You're better than I am at spotting these things.

"If necessary I will ask her outright. When I look at you, shake your head to warn me off or nod for OK. But I expect her to deny it even if it's true."

Amos instructed one of the constables to ring Austin's surgery to warn of their visit and to ask her to try to clear a slot between patient appointments. Amos drove as there was no desperate hurry and Swift tended to go a little too quickly for his liking. Besides, it was shorter to cut across country to Billinghay on minor roads en route to the surgery north of Boston rather than take the A15 and pick up the A17 at Sleaford, which would bring them too far south.

Swift sighed as they reached Metheringham and shifted her feet on imaginary pedals. She would have gone the speedy way. Amos drove on, regardless, with his customary cautiousness, and they arrived at the surgery to find a couple of patients waiting.

The receptionist was expecting them. Before they had time to introduce themselves she gestured towards a couple of empty seats and assured them that Dr Austin would see them as soon as she had finished with her current patient.

It was all done to avoid mention that this was an official police visit but Amos could tell from the surreptitious sideways glances of the two waiting patients that they knew perfectly well what it was all about. The patients sat in silence, staring ahead most of the time to avoid looking at the elephants in the room.

The delay was less than five minutes before the receptionist looked up and said: "Dr Austin will see you now if you'd like to go through. It's the door on the right."

Presumably patients exited out of the back of the building unless they needed to speak to the receptionist, for there was no sign of whoever had been with the doctor.

Dr Austin was putting a file into her out tray as they entered. She was seated behind her desk and there was just one chair opposite her. Amos, despite being the senior officer, was about to allow courtesy to outweigh protocol but Swift outmanoeuvred him by striding into a corner and rescuing a second chair which she plonked down on unceremoniously a fraction further back from that now available to Amos.

The doctor shuffled a few papers deliberately but aimlessly, apparently determined to be the one keeping the police officers waiting for a few moments rather than the other way round.

Finally she looked up and asked calmly: "What can I do for you officers? I rather thought I'd answered all your questions on Saturday."

"I'm sure you didn't think any such thing," Amos responded tartly. "You didn't, for a start, tell us you were Simeon Knowles's doctor."

Austin clasped her hands in front of her chest, leaned forward slightly and responded: "You didn't ask."

"I didn't ask because I didn't know," Amos said testily. He was as annoyed with himself for not thinking of it on Saturday, in the haste to get through as many interviews as possible while memories were still fresh, as much as he was with the doctor for not volunteering a piece of information that was obviously relevant and was bound to surface sooner rather than later.

Austin simply shrugged her shoulders.

"There you are, then," she said noncommittally.

Amos, normally a patient man, was beginning to get riled by Austin's attitude.

"Right, let's start at the beginning," Amos said. "Can you confirm that Simeon Knowles was registered with your practice?"

"Yes," Austin said thoughtfully. "I think I can confirm that without breaching patient confidentiality. Yes, he was."

"And you are the only GP at this practice?"

"Yes. I bring in a locum when I am away, which is not very often. I rarely take a holiday and I am never ill."

"And was Simeon Knowles often ill?"

"Inspector," Dr Austin said with an indignation that did not sound entirely natural, "I really am not prepared to discuss my patients – not even dead ones."

"For heaven's sake," Amos protested with genuine indignation. "This is a murder inquiry. I'm told that Knowles consulted you frequently. Was he ill or was he a hypochondriac?"

"If your source of information is so well informed on medical matters, perhaps he – or she – can fill you in on the details," Austin replied calmly. "For my part, I am not prepared to."

"A man has been murdered, cold bloodedly. Anything we learn about him could help us to trace the killer."

"I hardly think so. I shouldn't think there is much doubt what he died of. Anything that I know about his past medical history is just that, history. It cannot possibly have any bearing on the case, certainly not to persuade me to breach patient confidentiality."

Amos tried another tack.

"Did you know Simeon Knowles personally, apart from him being your patient?"

"I hope you're not implying anything untoward," Austin replied, leaning forward again.

Amos had, in fact, not implied anything untoward although the possibility was certainly in his mind. He was surprised that the doctor had seemingly taken offence so readily.

"Let's start with the entirely above board," he said. "Did you know Knowles socially?"

"Not particularly," Austin replied warily. "Everyone knew him in these parts, of course, and I bumped into him occasionally."

"But you knew him well enough to suggest that he take part in the abseiling," Swift interrupted. "When did you suggest it? I gather it was a last minute idea."

"I mentioned it to him quite some time ago, I believe," Austin said sniffily. "Several months ago. That was just a reminder when I told him a week or so ago."

"That's most odd," Swift persisted. "We understand that the whole event was dreamt up comparatively recently. You couldn't have known about it so long ago."

"Well I did," Austin said, leaning back in her chair.

"And you also suggested the bell ringing," Swift persisted. "Was that a recent idea?"

"I really can't remember," Austin said evasively. "I can't rightly remember whose idea it was. I think it may have been Mr Knowles who came up with the idea. He was all for a dramatic show."

"The chief bell-ringer and one of the other campanologists say you suggested it first."

"In that case, why are you asking me if you already know?"

"Because we'd like to know why you suggested it," Swift said with a mixture of exasperation and insistence. She wondered whether Austin was deliberately taking her down a false trail.

Austin shrugged her shoulders.

"It seemed like a good idea at the time," she replied nonchalantly. "It would attract a bit of attention."

"Or create considerable confusion, as indeed it did," Swift said. "Was that the idea? Why tell them to start ringing when they did? It proved very convenient for whoever seized the opportunity to tamper with the harness."

"It was a complete misunderstanding," Austin replied, leaning forward and engaging properly with the questioning for the first time. "I told them to ring later than they did. But that fool Herbert Townsend is always such a stickler for doing things by the book. They always start to practice the peal at the precise moment that the tide reaches its lowest point and that's what they did."

"Why did you ask for that particular peal?" Amos interjected. "It's meant as a warning of impending disaster."

"Well, it certainly proved appropriate," Austin responded drily.

Swift showed no sign of pursuing this line of inquiry further so Amos, a little puzzled, took up the cudgels once more.

"If you didn't know Simeon Knowles socially, and you decline to tell us whether he came to your surgery for medical complaints, real or imaginary, then there is one other possible reason why we have been told that he saw you frequently. Mr Knowles was, I understand, something of a ladies man. You're about the right age group for his tastes …"

Austin rose to her feet for the first time.

"That's quite enough," she said angrily. "You are not only slandering the reputation of a dead man but mine also. You are well aware that GPs are not allowed to have affairs with their patients. I could be struck off for it. You also know perfectly well that you have not a jot of evidence to back up that innuendo."

Amos glanced at Swift, who gave the merest shake of her head to indicate not to continue.

As the inspector rose to leave, Dr Austin pursued her advantage.

"I'm not angry for myself," she said in a calmer voice. "I can defend myself. But Simeon Knowles was highly respected, not least by the many people he has helped in their hour of need. I've no idea why you are treating this as murder. No-one would want to kill such a fine man."

Amos and Swift followed the exit sign and left by the back door. They walked round to their car in silence. Amos drove down the road and pulled into a layby where he was satisfied they could not be seen from the surgery.

It was Swift who spoke first.

"She was playing with us," the sergeant pronounced.

"By us, I take it you mean me," Amos said.

The absence of a direct response confirmed the answer as yes.

Swift went on: "She was deliberately trying to make us suspect her by being evasive. At times she was very obviously lying. We all knew perfectly well that I was making up the bit about the arrangements for the abseiling going back months and she played along with it.

"I think she's trying to protect someone by leading us down the wrong path. I can't see any other explanation for her behaviour. It would account for why she was trying to make out that no-one would murder Knowles."

Amos shook his head thoughtfully.

"I agree her attitude was strange, especially as she has to be the prime suspect. She was with – or at least near – Knowles all the time from when he put on the harness. Indeed, she had worn the harness herself earlier.

"It's true that several other people, some of whom we have not yet identified, had the chance to tamper with the harness in all the pushing and shoving but no-one had better access than Dr Austin.

"And as far as we know, there was no-one whom Austin would particularly want to protect, at least not to the extent of endangering her own freedom."

"What's the motive?" Swift asked, unconvinced.

"Sex as usual," Amos said bluntly. "I think she had an affair with him. If he finished it, that's a clear enough motive. No-one else seems to have wanted him dead. Right now, though, it's all pretty tenuous. We'll let her stew for a while. Let's get back to HQ."

Chapter 23

As Amos returned to headquarters, he spotted Sergeant Jenkins on the desk and stopped for a word.

"Good break?" Amos asked. "I gather you made it to Greece this year."

"Terrific," Jenkins replied enthusiastically. "The family loved it. Best holiday we've ever had. And the most expensive, but never mind. Even coming back to work hasn't taken the edge off it."

"What do you mean?" Amos asked, puzzled.

Jenkins beamed broadly.

"I've just heard," he replied with enthusiasm, "about Simeon Knowles getting his just desserts. That man was a complete bastard."

Amos looked at the desk sergeant in astonishment. This was the first word of criticism that anyone had levelled against a man who was supposedly such a paragon of virtue that no-one, except perhaps a jealous lesser mortal, could possibly have wanted to kill him.

"You didn't know?" Jenkins asked in some amusement. "No-one had a good word for him. I'm only sorry I wasn't there to scrape him off the pavement. I hope it's been disinfected since he splattered all over it."

The sergeant looked at his watch.

"Look, I'm on a break in 20 minutes. Why don't you join me for a cuppa in the canteen and I'll tell you all about it."

This must be serious, Amos thought. *Jenkins never discussed work on his break and would often leave the building and walk around rather than get drawn into a chat that would inevitable lead back to police business.*

Jenkins was a great believer that breaks were breaks, an opportunity to clear your mind. You came back refreshed and all the better able to do your job. He argued with some justification that putting work out of your mind allowed your brain to work on outstanding issues subconsciously. Those who found no escape in their working day, whatever their line of business, gradually functioned less and less effectively.

Amos readily agreed to the meeting. That gave him just enough time to check on progress, if any, in the investigation and see that members of the team were gainfully employed.

There was in fact some progress: a fair amount of information on the late Simeon Knowles had been unearthed. He was aged 71 and had lived all his life in the substantial house on the edge of Keele hill some 10 miles north of Boston, with clear views across to the Norfolk coast and easy access to the fens and the wolds.

He had inherited the family home from his parents but he had a younger brother and it was not yet clear whether his sibling had also inherited from the parents or whether any such division had been equal.

Knowles married at the age of 30 and there had been two children, a girl called Becky and a boy named John. The girl had married and emigrated to Australia. Word was still awaited from the Australian authorities as to where she was at the time of her father's death.

Mrs Knowles had died of a heart attack 10 years previously. The son had also died about five years ago from the same genetic defect that had killed his mother.

106

Knowles was chairman of the Fens and Wolds Golf Club situated further west along the ridge from Keele. Amos knew of it, though he was not a golfer himself. He found that the end of the stick was too small to guarantee contact with the ball.

It was not a highly rated course because most of the land that it ranged over was too flat but it suited moderate golfers with pretentions above their ability. Amos was well aware that among the pretentious were retired police officers.

Knowles was also treasurer of a Lincolnshire-based committee that sent toys to orphanages in Eastern Europe.

"Well done," Amos said appreciatively. "We now have a picture of the man whose death was apparently so widely lamented."

He was in the canteen five minutes before Jenkins and had a mug of tea for both of them on the table ready.

Jenkins was not, however, to be rushed and Amos fretted as the sergeant queued for a bacon sandwich. At last the two were sitting opposite each other, Jenkins looking very relaxed and not just because of his successful holiday.

"Tell me about Simeon Knowles," Amos asked simply as soon as Jenkins had settled into his chair. "I take it you knew him personally."

"Professionally," Jenkins corrected before taking a huge bite out of his sandwich. There was a pause as he chewed contentedly.

"Good bacon sandwich they do here," Jenkins continued. "Best part of the whole canteen."

"Simeon Knowles," Amos prompted.

"How could I forget the name?" Jenkins asked rhetorically. "I was a young constable, a couple of weeks on the beat, down in Boston.

"I saw this Range Rover shoot through the lights at red. It wasn't even close. I counted three seconds after the lights hit red to him crossing the line. He had plenty of time to brake on amber and there was nothing behind to run into the back of him if he braked sharply, which he would have had to do the speed he was going.

"I stepped out into the road and signalled him to stop. He damn nearly ran me over. I had to jump out of the way. Anyway, he did stop. He'd had to slam his brakes on to get round the corner but he was still another 20 yards past me before he came to a halt.

"I walked up to him as calmly as I could but I was pretty shaken, I can tell you. The bastard leapt out of his car and started lambasting me, shouting about was I trying to get myself killed. I was inexperienced and badly shaken up so I'm ashamed to say he got the better of me.

"I started stammering about him coming through the lights on red but he said forcefully that I couldn't possibly have seen what colour the lights were for him because I was too far back from the junction. By now we were some distance along the road and it was impossible to prove exactly where I had been. Also a car coming from the same direction as he had done was now stationary at the lights and he claimed it had been right on his tail, which wasn't true.

"I insisted on seeing his driving licence, which he produced with some reluctance, and was writing down his details when he came the old 'I'm a friend of the Chief Constable' stunt. He knew the Chief Constable by name – it wasn't Sir Robert back then, it was well before his time – and he went on about them being members of the same golf club, which he also named.

108

"He claimed that he had used his influence as Club Captain to get the Chief Constable membership of what was a pretty exclusive club and if I caused trouble I would be in for it.

"I told myself it wasn't worth the hassle, me being new to the job and all that. So I rescued as much pride as I could from caving in and warned him to be more careful in future."

"You've nursed that grudge all this time?' Amos asked. "That doesn't sound at all like you."

"Nor is it," Jenkins retorted hotly. "All that, I could have put down to experience and moved on. But the bastard hadn't finished yet. Despite me letting it go, he still complained about me to the Chief Constable anyway. He didn't know my name but he had made a note of my number, which I think annoyed the Chief Constable more because it meant someone had to look up who I was.

"And he complained about me in front of other golf club committee members, making the Chief Constable look small and jeopardising his golf club membership. So I got a lecture and a black mark right at the start of my career. I couldn't get promotion to sergeant until we had a new Chief Constable and by then it was too late to hope to progress to inspector."

Jenkins finished his bacon sandwich and downed the rest of his tea in silence.

"I thought I had a chance to get him some years later. I was in a patrol car when we got an anonymous tip off that he had left the golf club after downing a couple of gin and tonics too many. This time there were two of us and we managed to intercept him just before he got home.

109

"We got a lot of bluster and the usual threats about reporting us as he tried to waste time while he could breathe deeply and expel the alcohol. I wasn't bothered because he couldn't blight my career any worse and he was, to be honest, rather resigned to being over the limit.

"But his belief that he can break the law with impunity was not about to be shattered. He registered just a fraction below the limit. My partner in the car and I would really have been for the high jump but, to my astonishment, he didn't wait to take our names and he never did complain about us.

"Instead, he leapt back into his car, swung it round – which took a bit of doing in such a narrow road – and nearly knocked us over in his haste to drive back to the golf club. I learnt later that he fired the manager on the spot for watering down the gin."

Then Jenkins pushed back his chair and stood up to leave.

"The man was a real bastard," he said as his parting shot. "Don't let anyone tell you otherwise."

Chapter 24

Amos had hardly got back to his desk when his telephone rang. It was Gerry Burnside at Boston on the line.

"Where the hell are you?" Burnside barked out as soon as Amos answered. "All hell's broken loose. We're getting flooded out with calls, all asking for you. People are pretty narked when we say you're not here. Some refuse to speak to anyone else."

"Calm down, Gerry," Amos said, as soon as he could butt in. "What on earth are you on about?"

"Your TV show," came the answer. "It's all very well giving out YOUR name and OUR number just as long as you're here to pick up the pieces. What are you doing back in Lincoln anyway?"

What indeed, Amos suddenly wondered. *Why on earth hadn't he and Swift carried on to Boston? The one good thing about it was that he now had a completely new light on the character of the hitherto saintly Simeon Knowles.*

"You mean the interview with *Look North* went out?" Amos asked in surprise.

"It went out at lunchtime on the early edition," Burnside snapped irritably. "Don't tell me you'd forgotten about it?"

Amos had indeed forgotten all about it, given the distractions of events at home, at the doctor's surgery and then chatting to Jenkins. In any case, he had not expected the interview to be broadcast until that evening, when the pictures would also be published in the

Lincolnshire evening papers. Presumably the *Look North* producer had decided to steal a march on the print media.

"Sorry, Gerry," Amos said briskly, before remembering that inspectors had no need to apologise to sergeants, "we've been tying up some loose ends with Dr Austin and we had to come back to HQ to talk to Sergeant Jenkins, who had some personal knowledge of the deceased. We'll get down to you as quickly as we can."

Amos rang home to warn his wife that he would be working late but there was no response. Had she gone off to her sister's, like the last time?

Then he called Swift into his office so they could speak in private. In view of the incident with Swift's boyfriend Jason the previous evening, Amos offered his deputy the option of working on at HQ and getting home at a reasonable time that evening.

Swift promptly declined.

"I don't allow my private life to interfere with my work, sir, as you well know," she said curtly.

"That's fine," Amos replied. "It's just that Gerry is holding the fort down there and is keen to help so it wouldn't have been a problem."

Swift's face fell for a moment at the mention of Gerry Burnside but she swiftly pulled herself together and followed Amos to the car park, more determined than ever not to be usurped.

"In that case, would you drive, please," Amos asked, handing the keys to Swift.

She grabbed them eagerly. At least they would get to Boston in time to get on with the case.

Amos was deep in thought throughout the journey. He really had not been concentrating properly on the case. It was not just the strain at home, nor was it the fact that there was just one, obvious, suspect who was taunting him.

What was preying on his mind was the attitude of the Chief Constable. Sir Robert Fletcher had initially made it clear that he would have preferred a different inspector on the case because he wanted a quick resolution. Now he was now putting an obstacle in the way by blocking the post mortem.

It was more than just the post mortem. That in itself was insignificant, since even Amos did not expect it to throw up anything that he did not already know. It was more the growing suspicion that Sir Robert wanted the inquiry pushed back until it could be dropped quietly.

He no longer wanted a quick, dramatic arrest. He had not been in touch with Amos to see how the case was going. That would normally not have been untoward, especially when there was a pet campaign on the go. However, on the rare occasions when Fletcher had a personal interest in a case he would be continuously interfering.

The more he thought about it, the more Amos became convinced that the Chief Constable wanted him to fail.

Chapter 25

"Some names keep cropping up in the phone calls," Gerry Burnside said as Paul Amos and Juliet Swift entered the incident room, where three detective constables were taking the calls. All three constables were on the phone, scribbling away.

Burnside handed Amos several sheets of typed paper, some with additional notes in pen scribbled on as afterthoughts. As Amos glanced down the list, Burnside slid past him and edged a little more closely than decency would allow to Swift, who backed away as discreetly as she could.

Amos acted to distract the Boston sergeant.

"No offers on the couple in their forties, I take it, Gerry?" the detective inspector asked.

"Not so far," Burnside admitted. "Once we'd got names confirmed for the others in the photos we started asking the callers if they knew them but they can't be local. No-one saw them come into the church, or leave, and they didn't speak to anyone as far as we can ascertain."

"We'll start with the woman and child," Amos announced peremptorily. "They're nearest."

"A bit grisly, taking a child to watch a man plunge to his death, don't you think, Sir," Swift objected, while seizing the opportunity to move round to the other side of Amos, nearer the door and further from the attentive Burnside.

"I'm not thinking of her as a suspect," Amos conceded. "But she was there. Did she see anything? And did the boy see anything? Why have they not come forward?"

Burnside insisted that Amos and Swift take a burly uniformed constable with them to guard the car while it was parked. When they arrived at the house they understood why.

It was in a rundown terrace in a cul-de-sac with large potholes in the road, the odd brick lying around and a car jacked up on bricks with the wheels removed and the windows smashed in. There was no other vehicle in sight.

Eve German, the woman named by several callers, lived halfway down on the left hand side, though so few houses had numbers on that they had to start at No.15 and count up to 27 in odd numbers. The screwholes in the door that once bore this number could be seen among the peeling paintwork.

The window frame was rotten to the point where strips of newspaper had been pushed into the gaps to keep out the rain and draughts.

Amos knocked as loudly as he dared, fearing that a door panel would give way – just two raps with his knuckles. Almost immediately he heard running feet coming up behind the door, which was opened by the small boy in the photographs. He looked distinctly unkempt, with holes in his pullover where it was coming unravelled and short trousers that looked a size too small for him.

The woman who had been identified as Eve German by respondents to the TV interview hurried belatedly to stop him.

At least they had settled which woman on the photographs the boy was with, Amos thought, though it probably didn't greatly matter.

Amos stepped inside the door and showed his warrant card. The woman looked relieved. Perhaps, Amos wondered, she had feared that her visitors were the loan sharks who preyed on this area of Boston.

"Mrs German," he said, "we just wanted to ask you a few questions about the unfortunate incident at the Stump on Saturday. You were there at the time."

"Stephen, go up to your room and play while I talk to these people," the woman told the boy. "Stay close to the wall."

The front door had led directly into the front room and a door at the back was ajar, giving a glimpse of a kitchen containing a very old but remarkably clean gas oven and hob. In fact, as Amos glanced round, the front room was surprisingly clean and tidy. There was a small table with two wooden chairs and one battered armchair.

Along one side wall ran a steep staircase open to the room except for a rickety looking handrail.

The youngster left reluctantly but he kept to the wall as instructed as he climbed the stairs. German watched him all the way.

"You'll have to sit where you can," German said apologetically.

Amos pulled out a chair at the table and nodded to the armchair for Swift, so German sat at the table opposite the inspector.

"It's Miss German, by the way," she said tartly. "I'm not married."

"My apologies," Amos said. "Miss German, can you tell us please why you were at Boston Stump on Saturday morning with, I assume, your son."

"Yes, he's my son," German answered defiantly, as if she was being accused of having a child out of wedlock by a court of morals.

"The Stump," Amos prompted.

116

"We make our own entertainment here. As you can see, we don't have a television set, just a radio some kind person gave us."

"Was that person Simeon Knowles by any chance?" Swift asked from the armchair.

"No, it most certainly was not," German said indignantly.

"Miss German," Amos said soothingly, after looking at the battered radio which stood on the table between them. "We're not here to accuse you of anything or to pass judgement on your lifestyle. We are here because you may have seen something that will help us to determine how Mr Knowles fell to his death. So, do I take it you went to the Stump to see the abseiling as a free trip out?"

Slightly mollified, German nodded her assent.

"Did you know Mr Knowles or did you see anyone else you recognised at the Stump."

"No."

"When you went into the church, did you see a man wearing a harness? Did you go anywhere near him."

"I think I saw him," German said cautiously, "but I didn't go anywhere near him. There were lots of people milling around and the bells were clanging. We didn't stay in the church because it was so noisy and Stephen was frightened. We went across the footbridge to the other side of the river."

"Did you see a woman with the man wearing the harness?"

"I don't think so. I can't remember but there were lots of people."

"Miss German," Amos said quietly but firmly. "Why did you not come forward as a witness after Mr Knowles fell to his death? We were appealing in the local media for witnesses."

"We don't have a television so I didn't see your appeal," came the rejoinder. "And we don't take a newspaper either. I can't afford them."

As Amos opened his mouth to speak, he was interrupted by a small voice from the top of the stairs. Stephen had crept out of his room without anyone noticing.

"Are you here about evil granddad?" he asked.

German spun round in horror but before she could stop her son from saying more, the boy looked straight at Amos and added innocently: "He fell from the top of the tower."

Chapter 26

A shocked silence descended on the small front room where Miss German and her young son eked out a basic existence.

Realising he had said something he should not have done, but unaware of the bombshell he had just dropped, Stephen burst into tears and started to hurry down the stairs, sobbing "Sorry Mummy" and grabbing at the unstable handrail.

German leapt up in alarm and rushed over to hold the rail steady as her son half tumbled down the stairs and she hugged him tightly, reassuring him that he had done nothing wrong. As the sobs subsided, she carried him over to the chair at the table and sat him on her knee, still hugging him.

"Miss German," Amos said simply, "I think you have some explaining to do."

The woman nodded but waited for a few seconds until she was sure that Stephen was all right. However, she made no attempt to release her son.

"Yes," she finally admitted, "Simeon Knowles was Stephen's grandfather. I say 'was', not because Knowles is dead, but because he disowned us. He never was a proper grandfather."

"So Knowles's son was Stephen's father?" Amos stated the obvious. "Did Simeon Knowles know?"

"Oh, he knew all right," German said bitterly. "He knew."

She paused to look down at her silent and immobile son, clasped safely in her arms, and she kissed him lightly on the top of his head before continuing.

"John – that's Stephen's dad – and I met at a dance at the Gliderdrome in Boston one Saturday night. We really hit it off. John was working in a solicitor's office in Boston and doing really well. Simeon – and his wife – were really proud of him back then.

"They certainly weren't amused when I shipped up at their home one day. Their very-posh, everything-in-its-place home. They obviously thought I wasn't good enough. I'd come from a pretty lowly beginning. In fact, I was brought up in a children's home and went to the local primary school and then a comprehensive.

"I had to stand a fair amount of bullying to get to university and I had to work my way through to a degree with no help from anyone except the sympathetic woman who rented me a room.

"John had it all on a plate. But I didn't resent that. He was a lovely bloke, hardworking and considerate. He had bought a house with a mortgage in one of the better ends of Boston because he wanted to stand on his own two feet and not rely on his parents.

"They didn't like him leaving home but they accepted it because they had no choice. What they couldn't accept was me moving in with John. They were staunch churchgoers and they regarded it as living in sin. Finally, when all attempts to persuade John to break up with me failed, they refused to have anything more to do with him.

"John was very upset, even more so when his mother died soon afterwards. He and I were Christians in the true meaning of the word, not churchgoers but people who tried to live decent lives and help

120

others. We didn't believe in God and we certainly weren't going to get married in a church. We were fine as we were.

"I was teaching English in a school in the town for a couple of years and then I became pregnant. John was overjoyed and while it wasn't something I was counting on I was happy because he was happy.

"John told his father because he hoped that a grandchild would bring a reconciliation. He told John I was a gold digger and I had got pregnant on purpose to trap him. John was even more outraged than I was because he knew it wasn't true.

"Stephen was born seven years ago and for the next three years we were wonderfully happy apart from the sadness of being estranged from John's family. He had a sister who disappeared off to Australia and apart from his father he had no-one. I felt for him because I had no-one either.

"Then, when Stephen was three, John died of a heart attack. I have always believed that the strain with his parents took its toll. But for Stephen and me, the horror was just beginning. Have you read any Charles Dickens, inspector? *Bleak House*, where a brilliant legal brain omits to make a will, with disastrous consequences?

"John hadn't made a will. He died intestate. The house was in his name – he'd bought it before I moved in and I suppose the taunts from his father about me being a gold digger meant I never pressed him to put it into joint names. The car and his investments were also in his name only.

"You've heard the saying 'he'd rob his own grandmother'? Simeon Knowles actually did rob his own grandchild. He took everything. He went to court to get us evicted. That was another disaster. We left the house thinking the council would rehouse us but they said we had made ourselves homeless. It seems we should have waited for the court to appoint a bailiff to escort us off the premises.

"I had a bit of cash in the account I had when I was teaching so we managed to rent this ghastly place and we've lived off benefits ever since. I'm trying to get back into teaching now Stephen's a bit older."

"You realise this gives you a motive, and you were there when it happened," Swift said sternly. "Why did you lie to us?"

German made no reply. She was quietly sobbing, her son clinging to her.

"I think that's enough for now, Miss German," Amos said gently. "We'll see ourselves out."

Chapter 27

Jonas Tomlinson lived on the northern outskirts of Boston in a better area where homes were sparser but generally well appointed. However, this house, like Eve German's, had clearly seen better days. So, too, had Tomlinson.

Amos and Swift were shocked to be greeted by a thin, elderly man with unkempt hair in scruffy clothes and sporting three days of stubble on his chin. He had looked quite respectable in the photographs, shaven, hair combed and wearing a suit, albeit one that hung rather loosely on his spare frame and with a tie not properly fastened.

Had they met him in the street they would not have recognised him from the photograph. Even on his own doorstep, Amos felt obliged to say "Mr Tomlinson?" as a question rather than a statement of the obvious.

Tomlinson nodded and invited them in, without bothering to ask for identification. Were they so obviously police officers or was Tomlinson glad of the company? Amos wondered as he entered the front door.

While German had made a valiant attempt to keep the interior of her home in as clean and tidy a state as possible, Tomlinson had made no such effort.

The narrow hallway badly needed decorating. The wallpaper was dirty where people had rubbed against it as they entered and you could see the lines where the wallpaper abutted. Newspapers were scattered around the lounge floor and a plate and beaker stood on a small table. The television was switched on in the corner.

Tomlinson hastily switched off the mindless game show he had been watching, grabbed the plate and beaker and offered the officers a cup of tea. Swift, who had followed at the rear and had taken the opportunity of peeping into the kitchen unnoticed by Tomlinson, hastily declined and shot Amos a glance to advise that he do likewise. The detective sergeant had seen the pile of unwashed crockery in the washing up bowl and on the kitchen table.

"That's fine, Mr Tomlinson," Amos said. "We just want to ask you a few questions."

"Are you from the *Boston Standard*?" Tomlinson asked. "Is it about the drainage system?"

"Neither. We're police officers and we've come about the incident at Boston Stump on Saturday morning."

Tomlinson looked genuinely surprised but disappointed. His face fell.

"Oh, all right," he said lamely.

"Mr Tomlinson," Amos went on. "You were seen at Boston Parish Church on Saturday morning. Why were you there?"

"It's my parish church. I go every Sunday."

"But you were there on Saturday," Amos persisted. "Why on Saturday?"

"I live on my own," Tomlinson replied evasively. "I just wanted a bit of company."

"Enough to dress up for?" Swift said, with a sarcasm that was wasted on Tomlinson.

"I always shave and wear my suit and tie for church. It's only respectful in the house of God. Saturday's no different. I just don't bother much at home because there's no-one to dress up for."

"Shall we get to the point, Mr Tomlinson?" Amos asked impatiently. "You went to the Stump because Simeon Knowles was taking part in the abseiling, didn't you? So how did you know him?"

"I didn't know him. I'd never met him before in my life."

"But you walked up to him in the church," Amos exclaimed. "Are you telling me you walked up to and spoke to a complete stranger just on a whim, like you seem to be making out you just went to the church on a whim? And lo and behold, the man plunges to his death ten minutes later. A bit of an unfortunate coincidence, wouldn't you say?"

Tomlinson fell into a sullen silence.

"Let's start again," Amos said. "You did go to Boston Stump because of Simeon Knowles, didn't you?"

Tomlinson nodded his assent.

"Who told you he was going to be there. It was Dr Austin, wasn't it?"

"Not actually Dr Austin. Her receptionist phoned and told me about it. She said I should be there."

"Did she say why?"

"No."

"I think she did say why," Swift interjected. "I think she made it very clear that it would be worth your while."

Tomlinson went quiet again.

"Which brings us to why Dr Austin thought you would want to see Simeon Knowles plunge to his death," Amos took up the questioning again. "Why?"

"Nobody said anything about him dying. Just that he was taking part in the abseiling and to be there. Well, I was curious what it was all about, that's all."

"Why were you curious, Mr Tomlinson? How did you know him?"

"Everyone in Fens farming knew him. He had dealings with a lot of farmers."

"What sort of dealings?"

"Oh, you know, this and that."

"No, I don't know, Mr Tomlinson," Amos said in exasperation. His uncustomary impatience was developing into anger. Tomlinson got the message.

"He used to help out with money. For buying machinery or to tide people over."

"So for example," Amos asked, "if the harvest was late he's the man you would turn to for a loan until you sold your crop?"

"That's right. He was well known for it."

"And how much interest did he charge?"

"*I* don't know," Tomlinson said with a strong accent on the word "I". "I never borrowed from him. I wasn't a farmer," he said firmly.

Amos looked at him in blank astonishment. There were some inquiries where everyone seemed only too eager to cooperate and those where people were deliberately evasive for no obvious reason. This case was rapidly developing into the latter category.

"Did you have any kind of business dealings with him?" Amos finally asked.

"No. I'd no reason to. I didn't move in his league."

"So you knew him personally, then?"

"Not really. I was a member of the Fens Golf Club donkey's years ago when he was chairman. I have to admit he got things done. The place fell apart after he left to join a better club. I hear he went back again a year or two ago but I'd given up golf by then. My knee's about shot."

"So why on earth would Dr Austin think you would be interested in seeing Simeon Knowles abseil down Boston Stump? And more to the point, why on earth *were* you? You turned up after all."

"I don't get out much, only to church on a Sunday, and she probably thought it would do me good. And that's why I went."

Chapter 28

" Do you think we could find Hollyoaks Farm again?" Amos asked Swift. "It won't be much of a detour."

"You want to talk to Mrs Mason again?" Swift asked in surprise. "I can't think she's got anything much to add."

"No," Amos replied. "I'm anxious to know what her husband thought of Saint Simeon. In my experience, a lot of Lincolnshire farmers don't let their wives know everything about their finances, especially when they get into trouble. I just wonder what Steve Mason has to say."

Swift drove as they cut across eastwards to the A16, turned north then spotted the right hand turn that led to the farm.

"Go past the house," Amos instructed his sergeant. "With a bit of luck at this time of day we'll catch Mason in the fields. I'd rather talk to him on his own."

Sure enough, they spotted a man on a tractor in a field adjacent to the road. Swift was able to pull in through an open five-barred gate and park on firm grassy ground just inside the low hedge. They watched for the tractor, which had been moving away from them when they first spotted it but was sweeping round the field and was soon heading towards them.

Mason pulled up alongside the two detectives and switched off the noisy engine, which was emitting a fair amount of pollution from its rusty exhaust.

Amos produced his warrant card, saying "We're police officers" as he did so.

"I thought you were," Mason replied. "I recognised you from my wife's description the other day."

"I gather from your wife that you knew Simeon Knowles," Amos said.

Mason nodded.

"And you had some financial dealings with him?"

The farmer nodded again.

"Do you mind if I ask you about it? When was this?"

"It was a few years back," Mason replied. "It all seems a long time ago now. It was just the once."

"You borrowed money from him, I gather. You were a bit strapped for cash at the time."

"It was just a temporary setback. One bad year. The bank was being a bit difficult. You know the old saying that there's only one way to persuade the bank to lend you money and that is to prove conclusively that you don't need it."

"A few thousand?" Amos surmised.

Mason shrugged his shoulders noncommittally.

"Is that a yes?"

"I can't remember the details."

"You can't remember the details?" Amos exploded. "You get a lifesaving loan from a good Samaritan and you can't remember the details?

"I tell you what, Mr Mason. Do you think you might remember the details in the comfort of your front room? Perhaps your wife could help you to remember."

129

"There's no need to involve Irene," Mason said hastily. "She's gets high blood pressure. I don't want you worrying her."

"As you didn't with the details of the loan, I take it."

Mason nodded sullenly.

"So how much did Simeon Knowles lend you?"

"Five thousand."

"And he charged you interest?"

Another nod.

"More than the bank would have charged?"

"Quite a lot more as it turned out. It was all a bit informal and I didn't quite realise how much he was charging at first. I was worried sick about the farm and was trying to keep the extent of the problem from Irene so I was a bit distracted. And because it was done privately I couldn't set the loan off against tax.

"We just had to tighten our belts. It was more than a year and a bumper harvest before I could clear all the debt and I had to sell off some land even then but at least I got a good price for it. The Danes were just starting to buy up land in Lincolnshire. It provided us with some savings to invest in case we got into difficulties again. Irene doesn't know one half of it. Please don't tell her."

"I'm sure that won't be necessary, Mr Mason," Amos assured him.

"I've never had dealings with Knowles since. That man has lots of business acquaintances but no real friends. He does a lot of stuff for charity and they all turn up to keep the right side of him but they all pull him to pieces behind his back. There's a lot of talk about whether all the money gets passed on to the charities."

"Yet you went to the Stump on Saturday morning to support him," Swift interposed suddenly.

130

She was really pushing her luck, Amos thought to himself. Mason was not on the list of people named as being on the photographs.

Mason stammered a denial. It was impossible to say if he was telling the truth or bluffing. For the time being, there was no choice but to assume he was telling the truth.

Chapter 29

Paul Amos and Juliet Swift cut back to the A16 and headed towards Stickney for their next port of call. The woman who answered the door, tall, dark, slim and in her fifties, was easily recognisable as the second woman on the photographs that the American tourist had taken in Boston Parish Church on Saturday morning before Simeon Knowles fell to his death.

She had entered the church at the same time as Eve German and her son.

Amos showed his warrant card, introduced himself and Swift, and requested a chat about events at the Stump. The woman hesitated, then invited them in, peering round to ensure that no nosey neighbours were watching.

"I believe you are Mrs Rebecca Dyson," Amos said, after the three of them were settled into chairs in the front room. "I believe your husband died some years ago and that you live here alone."

The inspector had cribbed the information from notes provided by CID at Boston, gleaned partly from the phone calls from members of the public responding to the TV appeal and partly from the electoral register, which showed her as the only voter registered at this address.

"I am," the woman replied, "though I don't see what the rest of it has to do with anything."

Amos moved on without answering. Dyson was probably right, though it often helped to have as full a picture as possible of the person you were interviewing.

"Why did you go to Boston Stump on Saturday morning?"

"Why shouldn't I?"

"Mrs Dyson, you are surely aware that a man fell to his death from the top of the church tower that morning."

"Am I a suspect?"

"Not at the moment, though you're going the right way about becoming one," Amos said in exasperation. "We're talking to people who were there. Did you see anyone with Simeon Knowles – the man wearing a safety harness – in the church before he climbed the Stump?"

"I know who Simeon Knowles was," Dyson replied tartly. "He was a passing acquaintance."

"So did you see anyone with him? Anyone who could have tampered with his safety harness?"

"Quite a few people could," Dyson said unhelpfully. "Dr Austin wasn't watching him all the time. Quite a few people were milling about and some spoke to him but I'm not sure who. It was a bit chaotic."

"You went to the Stump with Eve German and her son," Swift interjected. "Why?"

Where on earth did that come from, Amos wondered, but he said nothing, for Dyson was clearly weighing up how to respond. Swift could have made the right guess. The two women and the boy had entered the church at the same time, thus causing temporary confusion over which woman the child was with. Only now from Swift's question did it occur to Amos that the three might have arrived together, that the boy was in effect with both women.

133

The sudden change of tack disconcerted Dyson, as did the keen stare of both detectives directly at her. Having no telephone and no means of communication, Eve German had had no opportunity to warn Dyson what the police did and didn't know. If Swift was right, the two officers had the advantage.

Finally she said: "Yes, I went with Eve and Stephen. It was company."

"You went right up to Knowles, didn't you? You were seen touching his harness," Swift said, attempting to pursue her advantage but overreaching herself.

Dyson spluttered indignantly.

"I never touched him," she said indignantly, "and neither did Eve."

"But you went up to him," Amos said, inferring that she had done so in the absence of a denial.

Dyson went silent.

"Mrs Dyson," Amos said gently. "We quite understand your reluctance to say anything that might look bad for you or Miss German but I assure you that neither of you are suspects."

"It sounded like we were," the only partly mollified Dyson said sullenly.

"We have spoken to Miss German," Amos went on reassuringly. "She has told us that she was the partner of Simeon Knowles's son and that her boy is Knowles's grandson. She admitted quite freely that she was at the Stump."

Dyson looked at Amos suspiciously but she accepted his explanation.

"Look, I persuaded Eve to go and to take Stephen. She was a bit reluctant but I believed that I could persuade Simeon to acknowledge his grandchild if we confronted him together."

"And did he?"

"No, but he didn't really have a chance with all the commotion. I was all for talking to him after he had done his climb but Eve said it was useless and she should never have brought Stephen. They left and were across the river when Simeon fell. It was horrible. I felt so guilty at talking them into being there."

"I suspect," Amos said deliberately, "that Knowles made it clear he would not relent. That is why Miss German didn't hang about."

"You don't understand. Simeon was a really sweet man, just a bit stubborn and set in his thinking. I could have talked him round if only I'd had the chance."

Amos looked at her quizzically. "Were you and he having an affair?" he asked.

"We had been out together a few times, on and off. As a matter of fact we were very much back on and he had asked me to marry him. I said yes."

"Off and on?" Amos asked. "And was it off at one point because of Dr Austin?"

Dyson blushed slightly and looked distinctly uncomfortable.

Finally she said: "Yes, Simeon and I did break up over Dr Austin but he came back to me."

"How did you come to know about Eve German and Stephen?" Amos inquired.

"Dr Austin told me about them."

Amos leaned forwards intently. "When?" he asked.

135

"A few days ago. She's my GP. I happened to be in the surgery and she mentioned it."

"And was it her idea for you to take mother and son to the Stump to confront Mr Knowles?"

"Well, yes … no … er, not exactly."

"How do you mean?"

"She did mention how wonderful it would be if Simeon made it up with them. Good for all concerned. And she did mention the abseiling event at the Stump but she didn't suggest I take Eve and Stephen there particularly."

"No, she just planted the idea conveniently in your mind."

"It wasn't like that," Dyson protested, but an element of doubt had crept into her voice.

"Let me guess," Amos went on. "She told you where they lived and encouraged you to make contact right away."

"Well, I suppose so, in a way."

"You must have been surprised to see the dump they were living in."

"Yes I was, but that only made me more determined to put things right, even when, as I said, Eve was reluctant. I'm sure I could have pulled it off."

"Are you sure you weren't blinded by love?" Swift asked. "We're starting to discover that Simeon Knowles was not the saint some people thought he was."

"No-one thought he was a saint," Dyson said with a laugh. "I loved him, yes, but it wasn't a mad, passionate, teenage love affair. He took me to nice places, places I couldn't afford. New Year's Eve at the golf club, charity balls, nice restaurants. He bought me expensive clothes."

"In other words, he bought you," Swift said disdainfully.

"No, no, he really cared about me," Dyson protested, but Amos could see that his sergeant had struck home.

Swift was looking round at framed photographs of Dyson and Knowles and others of Dyson on her own.

"Did he choose what you wore out together?" Swift asked. "From what I can see, your taste in clothes suit you better than his."

Dyson looked embarrassed but said nothing.

"How did Dr Austin feel about Mr Knowles returning to you?" Amos asked.

"I really didn't discuss it with her," Dyson said forcefully, as if anxious to take the conversation away from her own relationship with Knowles. "I think she was a bit peeved."

"A bit peeved?" Swift asked with mock incredulity. "I should think she was pretty angry."

Dyson fell back into silence. Amos felt that this was as far as they were going to get. He stood up, thanked the woman for her cooperation and led the way back to the front door.

Chapter 30

"That didn't ring at all true with me," Swift said as soon as they were back in the car. "Did she look like the grieving fiancée? I think it was all a façade to make it look as if she had every reason to want him alive and divert suspicion elsewhere, particularly towards Dr Austin."

"I think you're right," Amos agreed. "Surely Knowles's fiancée would have arrived at St Botolph's with him rather than with the estranged mother of a grandson he refuses to acknowledge. No-one has suggested that they saw Knowles and Dyson in an affectionate greeting.

"Taking Eve German and her son along may have been just a cover for being there. There was certainly opportunity but we shall have to find a motive if she is indeed our killer."

With plenty to think about, the two detectives set off for their next port of call.

Janet Sutcliffe lived further north, back towards Lincoln, several miles north west of Boston in flat open country not quite out of the fens.

"It's a handy location for getting to Simeon Knowles's home or to the golf club," Swift remarked. "Perhaps she'll turn out to be another fiancée."

Amos, in the front passenger seat, shuffled through the notes provided by the thorough team at Boston police station.

"According to the information we have, she was stewardess at the Fens Golf Club for two years up to about 18 months ago. It would be

138

interesting to learn why she left and what sort of terms she was on with Knowles."

The latter part of the journey was absorbed in the task of finding her home. Even with the aid of a detailed map it proved difficult. Brickhouses Lane was unsigned and unadopted, a rough track that was half soil, half stones.

They followed a small red car cautiously up the lane, dodging as best they could the worst of the potholes. It turned out that the driver was Janet Sutcliffe.

"You're lucky to catch me," she remarked, after the two police officers had identified themselves. "I work in Boston. I'm not usually back this early."

Amos looked at his watch. It was 5pm. They had got through a lot that day and this would be the last interview.

"We're investigating the death of Simeon Knowles," Amos announced.

"Yes, I assumed you were," Sutcliffe replied. "I've no reason to help you. He got what he deserved. Good luck to whoever did it. I'm not helping you to catch them."

"I'm afraid you are," Amos responded sternly. "You can do it here or at Boston police station, which will be considerably less pleasant. You had the opportunity to do it and from the tone of your remarks I take it you also had the motive."

The two stared at each other for a few seconds. Sutcliffe cracked first.

"You'd better come in," she said with bad grace.

139

Sutcliffe locked the car and, using the same bunch of keys, opened her front door and walked through into her lounge without looking back, leaving the officers to close the door behind them.

"I'll offer you a seat but not a cup of tea," she said abruptly. "I don't want to prolong this any more than necessary. I'll cooperate as far as I must and no further."

Amos nodded to show he understood, then asked: "You were photographed entering Boston Parish Church last Saturday morning, just before Simeon Knowles climbed the tower. Why were you there?"

Sutcliffe stared at the floor in deep thought for several moments before replying: "I went to see Knowles. And I mean see – not speak to – and for him to see me."

"And why was that?"

"I wanted him to see I was prepared to stare him straight in the face."

"How did you know he would be there?"

It was not the question that Sutcliffe was expecting. She had assumed that Amos would ask why she wanted to confront Knowles.

"There was a notice in the doctor's waiting room," she replied hesitantly.

"That would be Dr Austin, I take it," Amos said. Without waiting for confirmation he continued smoothly: "Did she draw your attention to it?"

"No, it was the receptionist," Sutcliffe responded, a little too hurriedly. "Dr Austin never mentioned it. The receptionist told me Simeon Knowles was taking part. She seemed very proud of the fact that someone who attended the surgery was involved."

"We understand that you went right up to him and touched him," Swift intervened.

Amos tried not to let his astonishment show on his face. Swift was really pushing her luck. They had no such information.

"I didn't touch him," Sutcliffe said indignantly, inadvertently admitting by inference that she had approached him.

"So why did you go up to him?" Swift demanded.

"I wanted to spit in his face. And I did. But I didn't touch him."

"And what prompted this display of petulance?" Amos asked.

Sutcliffe sat back and avoided his stare, realising that she was being drawn into saying more than she wished. Amos let the awkward silence continue to increase her discomfort.

This time it was Amos who broke first.

"You'd better tell us what happened at the golf club," he said simply.

Chapter 31

Sutcliffe swallowed hard and decided there was no point in stalling any longer. It was clear that Amos already knew quite a lot about her.

"I was manageress at the golf club," she began, "and I really enjoyed it. I'd run a couple of restaurants in Boston so I knew what I was doing. Though I say it myself, I was good at the job. You can see my references if you don't believe me.

"Then Simeon Knowles took over as chairman. I don't deny something needed doing. The place was running at a loss. It wasn't all that popular with serious golfers because the course was too flat and uninteresting so the membership was made up of sloggers – people who couldn't afford proper golf lessons.

"So the fees were pretty low, the greens were not kept in best condition and the clubhouse was shabby. It was a downward spiral. But the members were pretty decent people who made friendly patrons in the clubhouse.

"Then Simeon Knowles arrived. Apparently he'd been chairman before, many years ago, but had lost interest and rarely showed his face. Once he was back, he brought in his mates and quickly took control of the place. He really enjoyed lording it over everyone and no-one stood in his way because no-one else wanted the task of getting the club back on its feet.

"He turned it more into a social club than a golf club. We were pretty out of the way so I daresay a lot of members drove home down

142

the back roads over the limit. Funnily enough, your lot never stopped them. Knowles always boasted that he knew the Chief Constable.

"Knowles was always trying to impress his contacts – and that included bullying me. He would deliberately belittle me in front of them just to show how much power he had. I was just about getting to the end of my tether when he pulled a real stunt.

"There was some very expensive wine in the cellar. I think Knowles had bought it and laid it down when he was chairman previously. He tried to force me to sell it to him at a fraction of the real price. I couldn't do that. It would have meant falsifying the accounts. So I refused. He went ballistic – in private of course. No-one else knew about this.

"The atmosphere between us was so poisonous that a couple of days later he ordered me to resign. He said if I didn't go quietly he would see I never worked in Lincolnshire again. I didn't have much choice. I threatened to go to an employment tribunal but he said he would know the people on the panel and it would only make matters worse for myself.

"In the end I left quietly. I was paid monthly and I'd worked one week into the next month but he refused to pay me for it. He wouldn't give me a reference either. It took me some time to get another job and for a while I had to work part time but I'm finally back on my feet. So yes, I feel pretty bitter about him. I'm glad somebody got him."

"Did Knowles make advances to you of a sexual nature?" Amos asked.

Sutcliffe shook her head.

"No, I can't put that on him."

143

"In my experience," Swift intercepted again, "women who feel so bitter about a man have usually had a fling with him."

Sutcliffe was outraged.

"How dare you," she spluttered. "That man was loathsome. I wouldn't have touched him with a barge pole. I'm glad he's dead." Then, realising what she had said, she added quickly: "I've rebuilt my life and finally got a full time job again. I just want to forget I ever met him."

Chapter 32

The phone rang on Amos's desk first thing the following morning. When he picked it up, the inspector immediately recognised the voice of Brian Slater.

"You're in luck," the pathologist announced cheerfully. "I've got a slot, as they say in the airline industry. As a personal favour to you, I'm going to chop up old Saint Simeon. Someone's got to do it and it might as well be me. In fact, it has to be me since there's no-one else and there's nothing I like better than a nice martyrdom."

Amos was already on his feet, shuffling round the desk while holding the phone to his ear and having to lean forward as the telephone cord pulled tight.

"When?" he demanded.

"You want to see if his blood turns to wine or some such miracle? Better be quick."

Amos had not the least objection to seeing Simeon Knowles dissected at last. He would happily have wielded the scalpel himself.

"Don't start without me," he said.

"You've got five minutes," Slater replied. "And don't you dare tell the Chief Constable. He'll find me some paperwork to fill in for his latest campaign."

Slater had the naked body laid out on the slab by the time Amos arrived.

"I've done the preliminaries," the pathologist announced. "Height, weight, the usual stuff. Pretty average, bit of middle age spread but

145

remarkably fit for his age. No marks on the body except for the effects of falling from a great height."

Slater indicated the manner of Knowles's demise by raising his right arm and plunging it down sharply, fingers first, with a chuckle.

"No scars so I take it he's never had an operation. He looks disgustingly well – apart from being dead, that is. Let's see how many bones he broke."

Slater began his grisly work, whistling enthusiastically but tunelessly. He stopped cutting and whistling suddenly.

"I didn't reckon on that," he announced perfunctorily, putting his scalpel down.

"Reckon on what?" Amos demanded irritably.

"On cancer," Slater replied. "This is one nasty looking tumour. Wow-ee."

"He must have known about it, surely," Amos said, half statement, half question. Was the case about to close in dramatic fashion? Had Knowles committed suicide spectacularly and publicly? A last grand gesture to maximum effect?

"You realise this puts an entirely different light on the case," Amos went on. "It could be suicide after all if he knew he was dying. Wouldn't he have been in pain?"

"Not necessarily," Slater replied. "Cancer's a funny thing. Often there's no pain, at least until the very final stages. That's why it's so difficult to spot it early enough to treat it. He's probably had some discomfort, and felt listless, but not necessarily pain.

"We'll have to do tests to see how far its spread but I'd be surprised if there aren't secondaries. From the size of this tumour, he's probably riddled with it. You'd better ask his doctor. She must know if he's been in for tests."

"Dr Austin has some explaining to do," Amos said grimly.

Chapter 33

As soon as he was back in his office, Amos rang Gerry Burnside at Boston. Despite the initial decision to exclude him from the inquiry, it seemed somehow that there was no way of managing without him and he had a way of inveigling his way back in. Burnside could be very persistent, one reason why he was an effective detective.

"Gerry, Amos here," the inspector said quietly. "I've a tricky job for you. Are you up for it? You're entitled to say no."

"Course I am," Burnside responded with gusto. "Up for it, that is."

Amos had hardly expected otherwise.

"It may take you all morning," he said. "Are you clear?"

"I'm clear."

"I want you to go to Dr Austin's surgery but first I need you to ring up and find out from her receptionist when Austin will be leaving to start her home visits. It'll need careful handling but I'm sure you can use your legendary charm with the ladies."

"No problem," Burnside hastened to assure the inspector. "I'm nearer than you. I'll be there well before she's finished her surgery."

"No, no," Amos said hurriedly. "I want you to get there *after* she's left. She won't be helpful, even though this may help her. But I need someone she won't be suspicious of and she's already been interviewed by me and Juliet.

"Ring the receptionist and say it's nothing important but you just need to check something. In fact, you could say it's about the Chief Constable's anti-drug campaign and you need a bit of guidance. If the

148

receptionist asks, at least you can say you're not on the team investigating Simeon Knowles's death, which technically is true.

"Ask what time the surgery is likely to finish but in case you get delayed there's no need for Dr Austin to wait for you, it will do another day. Get there a bit early and park somewhere inconspicuous where you can watch for Austin leaving. And give her a minute or two in case she's forgotten something and comes back for it.

"In the reception are two filing cabinets with all the patient records. K is in the bottom left hand drawer according to the labels. That means you can get down to it while blocking off the receptionist so she can't stop you extracting Simeon Knowles's file.

"Get a quick look at it. I need to know when Knowles last saw Austin and whether there is any indication that either of them knew he had cancer. Cause as little fuss as you can, Gerry, and don't try to keep the file. I know it's a tall order and when Austin finds out and hits the roof, as she inevitably will, I'll take the responsibility."

"No worries," Burnside responded cheerfully. "I'm a big boy and I'm well out of Fletcher's firing line down here. I can take the raps."

"No," Amos said firmly. "That's not an option. The Chief Constable is interested in this case. Everything comes back to me. I hope that's understood, Gerry, otherwise you're off the case completely."

"Okay," Burnside responded reluctantly. "If you say so."

"I do say so. There's one other thing. If you can, ask the receptionist why she was telling the patients about the abseiling and encouraging them to go. Was it all patients or just selected ones? That's less important than the medical file though. Good luck, Gerry. See what

149

you can get. But don't attempt to remove the file. Just memorise as much as you can."

Chapter 34

Amos and Swift reached Boston police station to find that Burnside had already returned a few minutes earlier. Any concern that he had failed in the task was allayed as he triumphantly ushered them into his small office rather than the incident room where they could be interrupted by phone calls.

"I thought I was going to have to ditch the project before I'd even started," Burnside admitted. "Surgery was due to finish at 11 o'clock but I reckoned on it running beyond that – GPs always run late.

"I found a house near the surgery and persuaded the retired couple there to let me park on the front drive. Don't worry," he added hastily on seeing Amos's concern, "I didn't let the cat out of the bag. They thought I was watching for a lorry load of illegal immigrants being transferred from one field to another. They liked that, I can tell you, stopping them from pinching Lincolnshire jobs."

"Gerry, please get on with it," Amos said with exasperation. "You've obviously found something out so would you like to share it with us."

"Just setting the scene," Burnside said, a little peeved. "Anyway, I watched the last patient go in and the last two come out so I knew there was only Dr Austin and the receptionist in the surgery.

"It was another quarter of an hour before Austin came out and drove off. I was afraid she was waiting for me. Luckily I'd left orders that if she rang the station to see if I was still coming they were to say I'd gone off somewhere else on an emergency.

"Finally she came out and drove straight past me – and that's when I thought the game was up. She looked right at me as she came past and for one moment I thought she'd recognised me from the Stump on Saturday but she drove straight on so I don't think she could have.

"I wandered into the surgery quietly and there was no sign of the receptionist. It turned out she was in the back and she'd carelessly left the keys to the filing cabinet on her desk so I was able to unlock it, open the drawer and pull out Knowles's file before she heard me. I got a good look at it before she snatched it out of my hands and threatened to call the police until I produced my warrant card.

"Don't worry, I managed to placate her by promising I wouldn't tell Austin she had let me look in the files. I pointed to the notice about the abseiling that was still up in the surgery and she admitted that Austin had told her to mention it to people and had given her the names of some patients who were to be told to go. If they weren't booked in for an appointment the receptionist was to ring them up and stress the importance of being there."

Amos shifted in his seat.

"So what did you see in Knowles's file?" he demanded.

At last Burnside got to the nitty gritty.

"Simeon Knowles went to see Dr Austin about a month ago complaining of listlessness, which apparently was not like him as he was quite an active man. Austin noted that he was pale and had a slight temperature. She gave him a full examination and noticed that his lymphatic glands and spleen were enlarged. She took a sample of blood for analysis to see if it was an infection but the results, which came back three days later, confirmed her suspicion that it was leukaemia."

"I thought that was a childhood illness," Amos said, surprised.

"Not necessarily," Burnside went on, feeling rather pleased with himself and glancing across at Swift in the vain hope that she was suitably impressed. "We looked it up in Black's, the medical dictionary, just before you got here. Chronic lymphatic leukaemia can occur at any age from 35 to 80 so Knowles was well within the age range. It's actually most common in the 60s and men get it more than women. The prognosis isn't good, though the medics are working on new treatments.

"However, Austin did not tell Knowles he had cancer, definitely not at that stage. It seems that the good doctor pulled a few strings and got him into St Bart's in London for an MRI scan. Usually Knowles would have had to put up with an X-ray but St Bart's got this new-fangled scanner a few years ago and it's much better.

"Dr Austin got the report back last week, just a few days before Simeon Knowles met his fate. According to the report, he was riddled with cancer – a tumour in the stomach, an enlarged liver that is probably cancerous, signs of secondary cancer in his bones and small tumours on the brain. He probably had only a few weeks to live, if that."

"I can vouch for the tumour in the stomach," Amos responded. "I've seen it for myself. The big question is, had Austin told Knowles the MRI results?"

"It doesn't look like it," Burnside said readily. "At least not about what showed up in the scan. Knowles had not had an appointment between the scan results coming back and his death on Saturday. Unless, of course, Austin told him privately. But it seems unlikely.

She has recorded everything meticulously and there is definitely no mention of Knowles being told.

"I chatted up the receptionist and persuaded her to show me the appointment book and Knowles was booked in for Monday morning, presumably to learn his fate."

"Except fate intervened first," Amos said drily. "The trouble is, it knocks our one and only genuine suspect out of the frame. Why bother to kill him and face a lengthy jail sentence when she knew he would die very soon anyway?"

Chapter 35

Amos, Swift and Burns wandered despondently though to the incident room.

"Any news yet on Knowles's daughter Beccy?" Amos asked the detective who had been deputed to track her down in Australia.

"Sorry, no sir," the detective stammered.

Amos looked at him accusingly.

"We're not getting much cooperation from the Australian police and the time difference doesn't help," the young man protested feebly. "She and her husband have moved from the address we had and no-one seems to have a forwarding address for her.

"They think she has moved into an area where forest fires are raging and the fires are top priority for the police who are trying to prevent looting. Our missing person is small beer at the moment. I keep trying," the unhappy detective tailed off lamely.

A colleague came to the rescue by distracting Amos.

"There are some new leads, Sir," one of the detective constables fielding phone calls at Boston police station said. "I'm afraid they're anonymous but they are quite specific."

The officer handed Amos three sheets of paper. He took them and read out the gist of each aloud.

"Ask Jonas Tomlinson about his son – he borrowed money from Simeon Knowles. Ask Rebecca Dyson what her real name is. Ask Dr Austin if she was poisoning him."

"They sound remarkably similar in style," Swift commented. "Could they have come from the same person?"

"Two of them definitely didn't, because I took the calls," the constable replied. "One sounded elderly and the other much younger. I didn't take the third call so we can't be sure."

"Male or female?" Amos asked.

"All three female."

"I think we can discount the third call," Amos said. "We've just written off Dr Austin and there's no evidence that Knowles was poisoned. He certainly didn't *die* of poisoning. Come on, Juliet, let's take Tomlinson first, he's nearest and the reference is more enigmatic."

Swift needed no further summoning, for Burnside was edging uncomfortably close to her. She and Amos were soon in the car and heading back to see a man who, until now, did not even have a son as far as they knew.

Jonas Tomlinson was not on the telephone so there was no means of checking in advance but, as they expected, he was at home. He had said himself that he rarely went out much apart from to church on Sunday.

The man seemed surprised to see them again so soon but he welcomed them into his home nonetheless. At least they were company.

"Mr Tomlinson," Amos got straight to the point, "you didn't mention that you have a son."

"Had," Tomlinson said tersely.

Amos and Swift were taken aback.

"What happened to him?" Amos asked, rather less aggressively than he had posed his first question.

"He's dead. It's been five years now, but it seems like yesterday."

"Did he work for Simeon Knowles?" Swift guessed.

Tomlinson shook his head. "No, at least he was spared that."

"There has to be some connection between him and Knowles," Amos persisted. "You might as well tells us what it is, Mr Tomlinson. We shall find out sooner or later and you can save us a lot of time. If he died five years ago I assume he was an adult. What did your son do for a living?"

"He was a farmer, down on the Fens."

"How did he die? Was it an accident?"

"It was no accident. They said it was suicide but I don't believe James would have taken his own life. It's a mortal sin."

"How was Simeon Knowles involved?"

"He wasn't," Tomlinson said truculently. "It was nothing to do with him."

"Did Knowles lend him money?" Amos guessed. It seemed the most likely connection.

"I'm not saying any more," Tomlinson said. "Why should I help you to find Knowles's killer? No-one helped me when James died. Knowles got what he deserved. Good luck to whoever did it."

Chapter 36

"I assume Mrs Dyson, or whatever her real name is, will be at work," Amos said as they left Tomlinson's home little the wiser than when they arrived. "Perhaps she'll be more helpful if she thinks her colleagues will find out about her private life if she doesn't cooperate."

However, Rebecca Dyson's employer, the head of a firm of solicitors in Boston where she worked as a secretary, chose to be discreet and sent Dyson off to have a coffee break in the café across the road. The cafe was long and narrow so, with the lunch break not yet started and most tables empty, Dyson was able to steer them to the far end of the room where they could not be overheard.

"When did your husband die, Mrs Dyson?" Amos asked as nonchalantly as he could. At least the unexpected question threw Dyson for a moment.

"Two years ago," she blurted out. "But what's that got to do with anything?"

"Bear with me," Amos said reassuringly. "How did he die?"

Dyson looked dubious but eventually she answered: "Peritonitis. They rushed him to the Pilgrim Hospital but it was too late. Was that all?"

So this was one untimely death that could not be blamed on Simeon Knowles, Amos thought, assuming she was telling the truth about her past life. He decided to play her along a little before raising the question of her name.

"Did you and your husband know Mr Knowles back then?"

Dyson was noticeably relaxing. This line of questioning was obviously going nowhere.

"Of course not. He was way out of our league. We didn't go to the sort of places he did. I bumped into him when he came to the office about eighteen months ago. I was working on reception then. I'd only just joined and was trying to rebuild my life.

"Simeon wanted some legal advice and I booked him an appointment. We weren't his usual solicitors but he insisted he wanted independent advice on a stand-alone matter. Afterwards, when I left the office to go home he was waiting outside.

"I turned him down at first because I still hadn't got over Rob but I saw him again in Boston and we went for a drink. He was a perfect gentleman and didn't rush me but we started going out together."

"And did he dump Dr Austin for you?"

"No it was …"

Dyson stopped too late in mid-sentence. She took a gulp of coffee.

"Well, it wasn't actually anyone," she continued. "Not properly. Some woman called Rose turned up at my house one day and accused me of stealing Simeon from her. She accused me of going out with him while he was still seeing her.

"It wasn't like that at all. I didn't even know she existed. And when I told Simeon later he said she was a bit neurotic and it had been hard to tell her about him seeing me. He'd not told her straight away because he was worried how she would take it so he had to pick his moment. We hardly overlapped at all."

"Pick his moment or play you both along while it suited," Amos asked. "After all, he started to see Dr Austin before he finished with you."

Swift isn't the only one who can make great leaps of guesswork and hope for the best, he thought to himself.

Dyson was suitably disconcerted.

"Simeon was confused," she stammered. "He needed space. Dr Austin was more outgoing than me. But he didn't have an affair with her."

"Who told you he didn't?"

"Simeon told me himself. He said Dr Austin couldn't have an affair with a patient and he was on her roll."

"And you believed him?" Swift asked.

"Yes, of course. He did have a fling with her before he met me but he wasn't her patient then. He was quite open about it. He was cheating on his wife, not me, but his relationship had broken down by then. If he told me the truth about that, why would he lie now?"

Believe that and you believe anything, Amos thought. Surely Dyson was not so naïve? However, that was her story and she would surely stick to it, either because she did not want to admit to having a motive or because she did not want to admit to reality.

"Is Rebecca Dyson your real name?" Amos asked, suddenly and bluntly.

The woman sitting opposite was completely thrown. She had just taken a mouthful of coffee which she spluttered over the table, grabbing a paper napkin and clasping it to her mouth to minimise the damage.

160

"Of course it's my real name," she eventually stammered. "What do you think it is?"

"You tell me," Amos responded unhelpfully.

"Well I can't tell you," Dyson snapped. "Unless you're talking about my maiden name, and you don't sound as if you are, I've no idea what you are on about."

With that, Dyson extracted herself from her plastic seat and flounced out of the café.

Chapter 37

"I want to call on the Masons again," Amos told Swift as they stood on the pavement watching Rebecca Dyson return to her place of employment across the road. "I know we're trailing around a lot and not getting much further forwards but the Masons, I believe, are the only ones who have no apparent motive and are likely to give us reliable information."

Swift couldn't argue with that so she drove in silence up the stretch of A16 that they were getting to know so well.

This time Mr Mason was at home with his wife. He looked alarmed when he spotted Amos and Swift on his doorstep but the inspector smiled and held up his hand in a reassuring gesture.

"Please don't be alarmed, either of you," he said quietly. "We need some background information and you are our best bet. Please be assured that anything you say to us this afternoon is entirely between ourselves."

Mason seemed mollified and Mrs Mason was only too happy to be the centre of attention. Once more they entered the farmhouse's front room and made themselves comfortable. Mrs Mason offered to brew tea but Amos assured her that he wanted to speak to both of them together, which pleased her but disconcerted her husband again.

"Are either of you acquainted with Rebecca Dyson?" Amos began.

The Masons looked at each other, unsure what the inspector was getting at and concerned that they might land an innocent person in trouble unintentionally.

"We hardly knew her at all," Mr Mason finally said. "I don't think she had been around these parts for long. Not much more than a year."

"She must have been here at least a couple of years," Amos said. "Her husband died in the Pilgrim Hospital two years ago."

"Simeon told us they had only just arrived when it happened. He thought it was the strain of moving that killed him," Mr Mason said.

"Do you know where they came from?"

"No idea," Mr Mason said. "We hardly knew her, as I said. We just saw her and Simeon Knowles at one or two farmers' events."

"Were they an item?"

This time Mrs Mason answered with a light laugh.

"Of course not. Simeon just liked to have a pretty girl on his arm – usually a few years younger than himself. But there was never anything in it. Oh, he was very fond of her, everyone could see that. But it was purely platonic."

"Mrs Mason," Amos switched subjects, "you mentioned to me when we last spoke that Simeon Knowles helped several farmers financially but there was one he couldn't save. Who was that farmer?"

Mrs Mason hesitated but her husband said hurriedly: "I don't think it matters now, love. Did you mean James Tomlinson, Jonas's son?"

His wife nodded. "Should I not have mentioned him?" she asked doubtfully.

"It was perfectly fine," Amos said soothingly. "You've done no harm and we have spoken to Mr Tomlinson but he is naturally reluctant to talk about his son's tragic suicide and we were reluctant to press him too hard as he obviously has taken it pretty badly."

163

Amos hoped that was not stretching the truth too far. In reality he would have been only too keen to question Jonas Tomlinson further had he thought he would get anywhere.

"Of course," Mrs Mason said in a motherly tone. "You did quite right. Jonas was dreadfully upset and Simeon's death would have brought it all back. It was Simeon who tried to save James."

"By lending him money?"

"No, no. Well, yes, Simeon did bail him out but I didn't mean that. I meant when James shot himself. Simeon tried to talk him out of it."

"Simeon Knowles was there when he died?" Amos asked in astonishment.

"Yes," Mrs Mason went on. "It was just awful. Simeon had done so much to help him. He'd actually gone round to see how things were going. James was in the barn with a gun. He said he was shooting rats but he suddenly turned the gun on himself."

"Were there any witnesses apart from Mr Knowles?"

"No, there was only Simeon there. James wasn't married. He lived on the farm on his own."

"So that version of events was Knowles's?"

"Yes, of course. He was the only person there. At least James didn't die alone."

Mrs Mason looked puzzled, unable to grasp the implication of Amos's question, that the suicide might not have been as Knowles described it, that Knowles might have been in some way responsible for what happened.

Her husband had been sitting quietly, struggling over what if anything he should contribute. Finally, he made up his mind.

"I'm sorry, Irene," he said in a quiet, matter-of-fact way, "but it's time for the truth. Simeon Knowles wasn't the saint you and some other people seem to think he was."

Mason held up his hand as his wife opened her mouth to protest.

"Hear me out. It's true that Knowles helped us out in our hour of need but it wasn't done for altruistic reasons. He charged a very high price for his help. I didn't tell you at the time because I wanted to spare you from more worry. It was why we had to sell that piece of land.

"It's all right. We came through it, we're clear of debt now and we don't owe Knowles anything. Others weren't so lucky. And one of the unlucky ones was James Tomlinson.

"James got into trouble during the same bad harvest we did. Knowles was the only source of cash and he could dictate terms. James didn't own his farm so he couldn't do what we did and sell off some land. He struggled to pay off Knowles but with interest the loan kept getting bigger. Finally James was working purely for Knowles and making nothing for himself to live on.

"It was pointless. James had no dependents and no reason to go on. When Knowles called once more for his pound of flesh James ended it all. You bet Knowles tried to talk him out of it. Once James was dead he had no means of recovering his loan. Not that he did too badly out of it. The interest payments more than covered the original amount of the loan, plus a bit on top."

"How do you know all this, Mr Mason," Amos asked.

"Knowles told me himself. He wasn't averse to boasting of his achievements and driving someone to suicide was quite an achievement. He thought it would impress me how he could stand the loss of the loan, especially as he knew the struggle we had had to drag ourselves out of the mire. I have absolutely no doubt that Knowles was telling the truth. He was that kind of man."

Chapter 38

David, the Chief Constable's nerve-ridden press secretary and general dogsbody, was bouncing up and down as Amos entered the Lincolnshire Constabulary's headquarters in Nettleham, just to the east of Lincoln, the following morning.

"Sir Robert wants to see you right away," David told Amos. "And by right away he means right away. No sneaking off through the car park."

Amos, in fact, followed David willingly though with a little trepidation. Had the Chief Constable suddenly decided to take an interest in the case again? If he was hoping that Amos had got nowhere with the inquiry, he would not be disappointed.

However, the meeting was just as likely to be about the anti-drugs campaign that was Sir Robert's latest pet project. The quarterly meeting of the East Midlands chief constables was looming and it was Lincoln's turn to play host.

Amos preferred it when the meeting was elsewhere and Fletcher was removed from headquarters for most of the day.

It was not, however, about the anti-drug campaign. It was very much about Simeon Knowles and Fletcher was very much interested, for he even remembered Knowles's name, which was a rarity as far as murder victims was concerned.

To make matters worse, Brian Slater was already in the Chief Constable's office, looking sheepish.

"Where were you yesterday afternoon?" Fletcher demanded. "Were you working on the Simeon Knowles case?"

Amos looked at him in astonishment.

"Of course I was, Sir. You put me in charge, remember?"

"Don't be impertinent, inspector."

That was not good. Fletcher called Amos by his rank, rather than by his surname, only when he was really narked about something.

"And where were you working on the case?"

"In Boston and the fens, sir. That's where the murder took place and where people involved live."

"Are you trying to annoy me, Amos? I know perfectly well where the incident took place. But I gather from Slater here that it wasn't a murder at all. I see the post mortem took place without my knowledge when I had specifically given instructions that other cases should take priority."

Here Sir Robert Fletcher shot an accusing glance at Slater.

"However, I will overlook that – and the fact that I was not informed immediately of the outcome – in view of the fortunate chance that important evidence came out of it."

What on earth was Fletcher on about, Amos wondered. The Chief Constable had not the least interest in post mortems, nor did he ever wish to be informed of the outcome.

"Well?" Fletcher demanded.

"I'm sorry sir, I'm not with you," Amos blurted out.

"For goodness sake," Fletcher exploded. "Knowles had terminal cancer. It was obviously suicide. Throwing himself off the top of Boston Stump was the sort of grand gesture he was known for. No-one wanted him dead. Just wrap up the loose ends and we'll keep this as decently quiet as we can. If only you hadn't made such a song and dance about this in your stupid and entirely unauthorised television performance. David will have to limit the damage."

"Simeon Knowles did not commit suicide," Amos said emphatically. "For a start, he did not know he had cancer. He didn't know he was dying. And what happened to the knife used to cut the webbing? It was not on his body, or on the ground where he fell. Or in the church or on the stairs going up the tower. He could not have got rid of it. And finally, there were plenty of people who wanted him dead. If you'll excuse me, I need to go and talk to some more of them."

Taking the opportunity afforded by the Chief Constable being thrown completely off balance, Amos swept out of the room.

Chapter 39

"Burnside, for you," Swift announced curtly as Amos returned to CID. "He won't talk to me."

Amos, still seething from the encounter with the Chief Constable, nodded to Swift by way of thanks and took the proffered receiver.

"Gerry, yes, you wanted me."

"We've got another body."

Amos gasped. He had been convinced, without any specific evidence, that Simeon Knowles was a one-off. The whole circumstances of his death suggested that it was an individual case.

"Don't worry," Burnside continued cheerfully. "This one's definitely suicide. He was seen doing it and he left a note."

Amos suddenly cottoned on.

"By he, do you mean Fred Worthington?"

"The very man. The churchwarden who flitted around like a ghost. Well now he is one."

"Never mind the black humour, Gerry. I get enough of that from Fletcher. You'd better tell me what happened and when."

"About ten o'clock last night," Burnside said. "The two officers who went to the scene hadn't worked on the Simeon Knowles case and didn't make the connection. It was only when I came in this morning that I recognised him as one of the main suspects."

"Did he kill himself at home?" Amos asked impatiently.

"No. Worthington went down to the docks and threw himself in."

"How the hell did he get into the docks?" Amos asked with incredulity. "Security is tight. Who let him through the gate?"

"Take it easy," Burnside said. "It was all done legitimately. Worthington was a well-known figure at the docks. Apparently he'd got Viking blood in him. He spoke a decent smattering of Scandinavian languages so he often visited the docks to talk to visiting seamen as part of the parish's pastoral work.

"The security guard on the gate knew him well enough and didn't doubt his word when he said something had cropped up that he needed to deal with that night. He didn't know the something was suicide."

"So what happened?"

"He walked down into the docks and approached a ship that was coming in to dock. He waited for a few moments as the ship manoeuvred alongside the jetty then calmly stepped off just a second before it crunched up to the side. He was crushed between the ship and the jetty. No-one had a chance to save him. You can't stop a ship on a sixpence.

"They'd fished him out and laid him on the jetty by the time the police arrived about six minutes after the incident. It was a quiet night and the pubs weren't throwing out yet so we got a car there pretty quickly.

"Worthington had his driving licence on him so there was no difficulty in identifying him. He also had his insurance certificate with the registration number of his car, which was standing not far from the dock entrance.

"Two officers were despatched to the address on Worthington's driving licence, taking the house keys from his pocket. They didn't know if he had family or not. When there was no reply to the doorbell they let themselves in and found the place empty. The suicide letter was on the dining table in a sealed envelope addressed to Dr Austin, so they didn't realise what it was.

"They brought it back to the office and I took the liberty of opening it carefully so I could reseal it if it was perfectly innocent."

"What did it say? I take it you've got it in front of you."

"Of course I've got it. I'll read it out to you: 'I can no longer bear the burden of my many sins. I accept responsibility for what I have done. Do not blame yourself'."

"The burden of his many sins? Do people really write that stuff?"

"Apparently so. Worthington certainly did. Looks like his handwriting."

"Take a photostat of the letter, Gerry, then seal the original back in the envelope and pass it on to Dr Austin. Let's keep her guessing whether we've seen it or not. If one of your uniformed officers takes the letter to her it won't look as if it's come from the murder team. And for heaven's sake don't let the Chief Constable know about the letter."

Chapter 40

"We need to take stock," Amos said. "We're getting nowhere. We need to go through all the original statements taken at the Stump on Saturday to see if we have missed anything."

Burnside was all for joining Amos and Swift despite the tedium of what Amos proposed but he was called away on a local burglary where the intruders had threatened violence, much to Swift's relief.

Amos and Swift ploughed through the statements meticulously and silently, breaking only for coffee brought by one of the Boston detective constables.

Finally, Amos said: "Right. Let's draw up a list of suspects who had the opportunity to tamper with the harness and assess their motives. First, Dr Lesley Austin. She had the best opportunity of all but the least reason to do it, since she knew he was dying. Possible motive jealousy, as he seems to have walked out on the relationship at least twice, some years apart."

"There's also the possibility that she feared Knowles would report her to the General Medical Council for having an improper relationship with a patient," Swift added. "He didn't seem to care who he trampled on. But she seems to have rounded up people who had a grudge against Knowles before she knew he was dying. Was she hoping that if she goaded them one of them would take the opportunity to kill him?"

"That would tie up with her arranging the peal of bells," Amos agreed. "It created the opportunity for someone to think they could kill him and get away with it in the confusion. Perhaps the knife was meant for Knowles, not the harness."

"Could they all have been in it together?" Swift suggested. "Or have I been reading too many crime novels?"

"Let's move on," Amos said. "Next up, Fred Worthington, the phantom churchwarden. Motive, revenge for taking Austin away from him then dumping her."

"He seems to have taken his own rejection with resignation but it's human nature to feel more outrage for someone you love rather than for yourself," Swift said. "The suicide note is a clear admission of guilt."

"Jonas Tomlinson," Amos moved on. "Motive, the death of his son. Staging a dramatic death would be adequate retribution for him. It seems likely that whoever killed Knowles wanted him to feel terror, the sort of torment that James Tomlinson must have gone through before he put himself out of his misery.

"The we have Rebecca Dyson. Another wronged woman. Why is it that women are attracted to the worst sort of blokes?"

It struck Amos, as soon as he said it, that Juliet Swift might take offence at this remark, given that her own boyfriend was a thug on the rugby field and a wimp off it, but she failed to make the connection.

"I suppose," Amos thought, "that she doesn't see Jason as the wrong kind of bloke."

"It's quite possible that she had had enough of being messed about," Swift said. "I think he tried to control her, telling her what clothes she could wear and deciding where they went out. She seemed to be a trophy rather than a partner."

"Next, Janet Sutcliffe," Amos said. "Someone else whose life was made a misery by Knowles, although she seems to have got her life back together.

"And finally Eve German, forced to live a life of penury with her son while the boy's grandfather was rolling in money. It must have been pretty galling."

"Could she have hoped to gain from his death?" Swift wondered. "Presumably all the estate goes to Knowles's daughter, wherever she is."

"I think we can discard Mr and Mrs Mason as suspects," Amos continued. "There doesn't seem to be any real bitterness there, they've moved on from their dealings with Knowles and no-one has placed either of them at the Stump.

"Finally, I think we have to consider Herbert Townsend, the chief bell-ringer. He caused the turmoil that allowed the murderer to strike. He could have provided the opportunity for himself. If so, we shall have to work on finding a motive. We don't have one so far."

Chapter 41

Amos entered his house that evening to find a suitcase in the hall and the sound of the television emanating from the living room. Mrs Amos was back.

The inspector looked in, only his head appearing round the door as he gauged his wife's mood.

Mrs Amos looked up and said in a matter-of-fact fashion: "Put my case on the bed in the spare room, please. I'll unpack in the morning."

Amos readily did as he was bid. Putting the suitcase on the spare bed meant that bed would not be used that night.

When he returned downstairs, his wife was in the kitchen switching on the oven.

"I've put a couple of fish pies in from the supermarket. They'll have defrosted by now so they'll only take half an hour. We'll have frozen peas with them to save bother if that's all right."

Amos nodded to indicate that is was indeed all right. As long as he didn't put his foot in it, the domestic crisis was over – until the next time.

"How was Eileen?" Amos asked, referring to his wife's sister. This was safe territory.

"Fine," came the reply. "Never ails anything. Unlike poor Jane."

Amos looked quizzically. Should he know who Jane was? They knew several Janes.

"You know," Mrs Amos said irritably. "My old school friend who lives near Eileen. Or did. She's died of a heart attack. I'll be going to the funeral when it's arranged."

"When did she die?" Amos asked, anxious to make amends for not knowing which Jane it was by showing some interest.

"While I was there. Thank goodness I had the chance to see her before it was too late. She always caught whatever was going round but you wouldn't have known she was ill to look at her. It just goes to show."

Amos was not sure what it went to show, but he had a nagging feeling that it went to show something significant.

Mrs Amos spoke about her visit while they ate, then they watched TV. It was only as they were making moves to retire for the night that she asked how the case was going.

"We'll be making an arrest tomorrow," Amos said. "I can think straight when you're about. We've been seeing this case entirely the wrong way round."

Chapter 42

Mrs Amos was surprised to be offered breakfast in bed next morning. She was tempted to ask if her husband was trying to make amends for the cause of their temporary separation but that was against the rules so she simply expressed an interest in porridge.

Amos put the pan of oats and milk onto the small ring on top of the stove and gave the mix a casual stir. He brewed two beakers of tea, making no attempt to coordinate the culmination of his efforts as he did when he was in a hurry.

Thus there was time to take one beaker up to his wife and return to the kitchen in good time to give the porridge a final stir before reaching down the syrup.

"I thought you'd be off bright and early this morning," Mrs Amos said. "I thought you had a murderer to arrest."

"There's no rush," Amos replied genially. "No-one will be disappearing. No-one but you knows we've cracked the case."

"Not even Juliet?"

"Not even Juliet. You'll excuse me if I have mine downstairs, I hope. I'd better get this over with, even so."

Amos neglected to mention the real reason why he was in no hurry. Having had a good night's sleep to allow his brain to work on the finer points of the case subconsciously, he now needed to think through how he was going to handle the arrest.

He was not at all sure how things would pan out. Much would depend on the reaction of the murderer.

Eventually Amos pulled himself together and set off for headquarters to pick up the unsuspecting Detective Sergeant Juliet Swift. He outlined his intentions to her on the journey south eastwards. The inspector was not one to keep his conclusions to himself. If he dropped down dead or walked in front of a bus the criminal would not get away with it.

Then silence reigned until they pulled up outside Dr Austin's surgery.

"Go round the back and come in through the exit when the next patient comes out. Be on guard – Dr Austin may try to make a break for it."

Swift opened her mouth to speak but Amos was already striding towards the front door of the surgery. Rather than address the back of his head, Swift walked briskly round the side of the building to wait patiently at the rear exit.

Two or three minutes later a patient emerged from the rear exit, which could only be opened from the inside, and Swift caught the door before it could close. As she entered, Dr Austin emerged hurriedly from her room and turned as if to escape through the back, only to gasp audibly as she caught sight of Swift.

As Austin hesitated, Amos emerged behind her from the waiting room.

"Shall we talk, Dr Austin. I've told your receptionist not to send any more patients through."

Cornered, the doctor turned back into her room and sat behind her desk, breathing deeply and slowly.

"It's like this, Dr Austin. Many people felt like killing Simeon Knowles, for all his saintly image, but no-one actually summoned up the courage or commitment to do so. Until last Saturday.

"You seemed to go out of your way to make us suspect you, being devious when you could so easily have cleared your name from the start. I couldn't work out whether you were the murderer or whether you were trying to protect someone else. Or perhaps you didn't know who the murderer was but you just wanted to obstruct the inquiry.

"Either way, you were happy for Knowles to be dead and for the perpetrator to get away with it. So you must have really hated Simeon Knowles at the end."

Amos paused to see the doctor's reaction. She was listening intently but showed no signs of reaction.

"Shall I continue? At first I was convinced that you had committed the murder yourself and that you were playing a game of double bluff. I had no doubt that you had an affair with Simeon Knowles while he was a patient.

"Then he dumped you, as he jilted the other women in his life, including the ones he was carrying on with while his wife was still alive. That was enough of a motive. Or perhaps he also threatened to report you to the medical authorities who take a dim view of affairs with patients. They regard it as a bigger crime than being a bad doctor.

"Then we discovered, as you intended us to find out at some point, that you knew Knowles was dying. You were the one person with a grudge against him who knew there was no point in bumping him off. So who were you protecting?

"And of all the suspects, it seemed that only Fred Worthington fitted the bill. Worthington, another man you had an affair with, who you dumped for Saint Simeon, and who was still in love with you. Did you feel some pangs of guilt over the way you treated him? Enough to want to help him in his hour of need?"

Amos paused again to see what reaction he was getting from Austin. Some of what he was saying was speculation, some guesswork, but he was satisfied that he was on the right track. He looked the doctor squarely in the face but Austin simply sat and listened. At least she was not disputing anything.

"I don't think so. Everything came back to you. You were the one who got people there to the event. People who wished Simeon Knowles dead. Was that because you wanted to create plenty of suspects to take attention away from you? Or were you giving them the pleasure of seeing Knowles die so spectacularly? Probably a bit of both.

"You were the one who organised the bell ringing that caused such chaos. It must have been very carefully timed to catch you and Knowles on the staircase. You had only two or three minutes leeway.

"There was just one little problem. Why would you kill a man who you knew was dying? Why risk everything for no good purpose? And then it dawned on me. That was, in fact, the reason for killing him.

"You, like several others, felt like killing him but hadn't had the guts to do it. Then, suddenly, you were faced with the prospect of never being able to do it. Time was running out. You hadn't told Knowles he had cancer yet, had you? Here was the one and only chance you were going to have of letting him know the terror of looking into the face of his murderer, knowing he was about to plunge to his doom and there was nothing in those couple of panic stricken seconds that he could do to prevent it.

"He didn't know he was living under a death sentence anyway. He died wanting to live."

Dr Austin clapped sarcastically.

"Not bad," she said patronisingly. "Not bad. Yes, I came to hate Simeon Knowles, as most people who knew him for long enough did eventually. He was nasty, manipulative and vindictive. I left Fred Westerham to be with him and broke Fred's heart.

"Then Knowles dumped me for Rebecca Dyson. She was younger and prettier than me and hard up so she was flattered and grateful when Knowles took her to expensive places and bought her expensive clothes. He bought the meals. He bought the clothes. He bought her.

"When I confronted him he laughed in my face. He told me that if I caused trouble he would have me struck off. And to cap everything I had to suffer him coming to my surgery because he was still a patient. Mercifully he didn't come often because he kept pretty fit.

"It all festered but, as you rightly say, I hadn't the guts to kill him, though I want to do as much for Fred's sake as mine. And then I discovered it was now or never. I didn't intend to incriminate anyone else, not at first. I just invited them along to enjoy the show. And no, the timing on the peal of bells was not spot on. I meant them to start ringing just as Knowles went over the parapet. It was a genuine misunderstanding that caused them to ring out five minutes early.

"I gave the bell-ringers a precise time to start but I made the mistake of telling them it was low tide, which is when they always practice *The Brides of Mavis Enderby*. That fool looked up low tide, which was five minutes earlier than I said, and started then.

"That was when I realised I could get away with it. So many people with a grudge against him, all milling round with the chance to tamper with the harness. On the way up I slipped the knife into the bell-ringers chamber, which was now empty as the bell-ringers had all gone off with a flea in their ear.

"Poor Fred removed it for me and got rid of it. My one regret in all this is that his conscience got the better of him. I destroyed him twice over." Dr Austin lifted up her doctor's bag, saying: "There's just one more thing."

She clicked open the catches and before Amos or Swift could grab her across the desk she pulled a hypodermic needle from the back, jabbed it into her arm and pushed in the plunger.

Amos had reacted faster of the two detectives but he stopped halfway across the desk and made no attempt to pull out the needle. Instead, he slowly sank back into his chair.

"I'll get an ambulance," Swift gasped but Amos put a restraining hand on her arm.

"No rush," he said coldly. "We've no idea what was in the syringe. Let her go."

Swift sat back in astonishment.

After a couple of minutes of silence as the three sat staring at each other, Amos finally said: "OK, ask the receptionist to send for an ambulance. I think we've waited long enough to make sure."

They had indeed. Dr Austin slumped forward onto the desk in a coma just as the ambulance arrived.

As the ambulance crew carried the stricken doctor out, Amos said quietly to Swift: "It's better this way. There was nothing we could prove."

Chapter 43

Sergeantt Blackbourne was on the front desk when Amos returned to HQ.

"David asked to be informed as soon as you returned," he told the detective inspector apologetically. "I'll have to let him know."

For David, read Chief Constable Sir Robert Fletcher, Amos thought. The nervy, excitable press officer only ever did his master's bidding. Still, we might as well get it out of the way and put the case behind us. At least there was a successful outcome, even if it didn't turn out to be the one Fletcher had wanted.

"Go ahead," he told the sergeant. "I'll be in CID."

Sure enough, David appeared at Amos's shoulder a few moments later in an unusually cheerful and relaxed mood. This could be because he knew Amos was in serious trouble and about to get the bullet or be moved out of harm's way to traffic or Scunthorpe.

"No need for you to come," Amos told Swift, partly to spare the detective sergeant if it was trouble and partly to spare himself if he was to have ignominy heaped on him.

"No, no," David insisted but with good humour. "The Chief Constable wants to see you both. He was quite specific."

That was probably a good sign, Amos thought, as far as you could tell. Fletcher was unlikely to spread the blame for anything between two officers if he could put it all on Amos.

Fletcher was shuffling through some papers as Amos and Swift entered, a familiar tactic to make himself look busy. But he looked up immediately and put the papers down. Amos breathed an almost audible sigh of relief. That was a really good sign. Fletcher always kept miscreants waiting to put them in their place.

"Ah, Paul, Juliet," he beamed genially. "Come in, come in."

There were three levels of address from the Chief Constable. Your rank meant you were in serious trouble; your surname meant you were in mild trouble; first names were undiluted good news.

"Very well done on wrapping up the Simeon Knowles case," Fletcher continued enthusiastically. "I've just heard the good news from Boston. And the culprit has been pronounced dead at the Pilgrim Hospital so we are spared the cost and distraction of a trial.

"The best outcome all round, without a doubt. Who knows what might have come out in a trial anyway? Knowles had a lot of powerful friends in the county, you know. Least said, soonest mended, and all that."

Including some powerful friends in the police, no doubt, Amos thought, but his reflections of the case were quickly cut short by Fletcher.

"Paul, I'd like your opinion on this press release," the Chief Constable said. "I'm pleased to say that yesterday the region's chief constables agreed to a concerted effort in stamping out drug taking, a matter dear to my heart."

Amos looked through the statement and suggested one or two tweaks, more to show willing than to seriously improve the press release. David was actually very skilled at writing press releases and Amos said so. There was no harm in making one sincere comment among this show of hypocrisy.

*

185

There was one further twist to the story. Almost a year later, as Paul Amos and his wife managed to venture into Lincoln shopping for Christmas presents, undiverted by a telephone call hauling the inspector off to work, Amos spotted Eve German, alone but laden with carrier bags, emerging from under the ancient arch that formed Stonebow.

It was German who recognised Amos first.

"Inspector," she called out cheerfully, "You see me in better circumstances than you did before."

Amos introduced her to his wife and asked what had happened in the intervening months.

"I got a letter from a solicitor in Boston asking me to visit their offices. My heart sank when I got it because I assumed it was about some debt I'd run up and couldn't pay but it said I would hear something to my advantage so I thought there was nothing to lose.

"It turned out that Simeon Knowles's daughter in Australia had died of a heart attack. Apparently it was something genetic – his wife and son suffered the same fate, as I think you know. Luckily for me she died just before her father and she had no children, so Stephen was his only living relative.

"I'd put his father's name on the birth certificate so all the estate came to Stephen to be held in trust. The trustees agreed I could sell the house, which was far too big for us, and buy a smaller place in Lincoln in Stephen's name. They also negotiated to clear my debts at a reduced rate to give Stephen a secure future.

"We had no real friends in Boston and Stephen was unhappy at his local school so he was content to move. He's settled into his new school really well and, as you can see," she said holding up the shopping, "we are about to have our first real Christmas in years."

"Simeon Knowles seems to have done more good dying than he did living," Amos remarked to his wife as Eve German sailed off down the High Street.

"It's the sign of a saint," his wife replied dryly. "They work miracles once they are dead."

Printed in Great Britain
by Amazon

79719271R00109